aptop #2

double take

Things are Not What They Seem

by Christopher P.N. Maselli

Zonder**kidz**

To Children's Pastor Van Walker,
without whom the QoolQuad
wouldn't play sports nearly as well

Zonder**kidz**™

The children's group of Zondervan

www.zonderkidz.com

Double Take
Copyright 2002 by Christopher P. N. Maselli

Requests for information should be addressed to:
Grand Rapids, Michigan 49530

ISBN: 0-310-70339-5

Editor: Gwen Ellis
Interior design: Beth Shagene and Todd Sprague
Art direction: Jody Langley

Printed in the United States of America

05 /❖ DC/ 5

contents

Caught Red-Handed

1

The thing about destiny is that sometimes it takes a ninety-degree turn when you least expect it. One moment a man thinks he owns the world; the next moment, he discovers it owns him. For most, this would be a tragedy. But for one man, this was inconsequential. He didn't mind being owned by the world, so long as everyone else thought he was still in control. But that's when destiny stepped in with a ninety-degree turn and changed everything.

"Peee-uu!"

The Enisburg Junior High boys' locker room smelled like a combination of sweat and athlete's foot, but it was the perfect place to hide. During sixth period, no one ever used it—except for today. Thirteen-year-old Matt Calahan sat on a wooden bench between two rows of gray lockers, his laptop fired up in front of him. Matt's good friends, Lamar and Gill, were there, too—they had to be, or Matt was sure the plan wouldn't work.

"You sure the video camera's facing the right direction?" Matt asked Gill yet one more time.

Gill was still holding his nose. "Matt, you worry too much," he said, sounding like a duck. "I took care of everything."

"Well, I hope so, because this may be our only chance to prove that Coach Plymouth is innocent."

"The truth will come out," Lamar interjected. "I've known Coach long enough to know he didn't change anyone's grades just to keep 'em playing sports. Someone else is doing it, I'm sure. They're just letting Coach take the rap."

"I hope you're right." Matt ran his hand through his thick black hair.

Lamar tapped a locker with his fingertips. "I'll keep praying."

Matt checked his watch, then stood and peeked around the row of lockers. He spied the entrance to Coach Plymouth's office. "Alfonzo should be coming by any minute."

"You bring an extra battery?" Gill asked.

"Of course," Matt said. "You sure you got the camera hooked up to the closed-circuit TV system correctly?"

Redheaded Gill lifted up his hands and held them out dramatically.

"Sorry," Matt apologized. "Just making sure."

Just two class periods ago, in his media elective, Gill had wheeled the AV department's video camera into the coach's office. The plan? He would fulfill his media class assignment by interviewing Coach about the upcoming basketball season . . . but then he would leave the camera in the coach's office, hooked up to the closed-circuit TV system. And so, when Alfonzo came by two periods later to work with Coach on his basketball moves in the gym, that would leave the office empty. Perhaps *then* they could catch the grade-changer red-handed . . . for the entire school to see.

So far so good. Well, *pretty* good. Gill's interview with the coach hadn't gone so well. While Gill loved being in front of a camera, his interview skills needed some improvement. The entire interview went something like:

Gill: Hey, Coach! How are you doing?

Coach: Good.

Gill: Good. Me, too.

Coach: Good.

Gill: So are you looking forward to the upcoming basketball season?

Coach: Yep.

Gill: Me, too.

Coach: Good.

Gill: So how do you think it'll be?

Coach: Fine.

Gill: Good.

And so forth. Matt was sure his friend wouldn't be winning the Pulitzer anytime soon.

"This better be fast," Lamar urged, his brown eyes connecting with Matt's. "We can't stay out of study hall forever."

"You guys should sign up for the AV department," Gill offered. "We get all kinds of time to wander the halls. We even hear about drama stuff before everyone else. Like I just read that they're holding auditions for a commercial downtown. I might go."

"You're going to be on TV?" Lamar asked.

"Well, I might audition. The world needs to see my talent. This time next month, I could be famous."

A low whistle echoed in the locker room.

"Great!" Matt exclaimed. "That's Alfonzo. He's going to get Coach out." He rubbed his hands together. "Gill, go watch and tell me when they leave."

"Right!" Gill said and disappeared around the corner.

Lamar let out a low breath. Matt thought Lamar seemed just about as nervous as he was. Of course, this was the first time they were using the laptop to solve a crime. Sure, they had stopped a bank robbery, but this was real Hardy Boys stuff. They had done their homework, and now they were hoping they had come to the right conclusion. If their plan worked, Matt's amazing laptop would save the day once again and Coach would be vindicated.

Matt had received the laptop a few weeks prior, on his thirteenth birthday. It was the best present his parents had ever given him. For a long time, he'd wanted to ditch his paper and pens and write like a *real* writer—with a keyboard and monitor. What his parents didn't know—and what he soon found out—was that his laptop had . . . well . . . "special abilities." Quite simply, Matt, Lamar, Gill, and Alfonzo had discovered that Matt could change the future with the words he typed on his laptop. The boys vowed to keep this discovery a secret; they had to protect the laptop from falling into the wrong hands. But they also saw the enormous potential in this particular birthday gift. And so they made another vow—they would use Matt's laptop to make dreams come true. Or, in this case, to solve a mystery so that the truth would be known. Because as Lamar always said, "When God gives you a gift, you gotta use it."

A moment later, Gill came racing back.

"They left!"

"They left?"

"They left!"

"Good! Let's get started."

Gill ran off again and Matt wiggled his fingers, placing them on his laptop's keyboard. He typed:

> Shortly after Coach left his office, the grade-changer chuckled. He knew he had this grade-changing thing in the palm of his hands. It was too easy—nudging those grades over the top, doing the whole school a gigantic favor . . . all the while letting Coach Plymouth take the rap. Bad grade-changer! Bad! But he didn't care. He was a crafty one.

"Maybe a little less editorializing," Lamar suggested.

Matt tipped his head toward Lamar. "I have to get the creative juices flowing."

Matt continued.

> At once, the grade-changer left wherever he was. He knew the heat was on Coach and he wanted to double-check . . . to make *sure* the grades he'd altered hadn't been changed back. He needed them changed.

"What if it's a girl?"

"A girl?"

"Yeah, what if a girl is changing the grades? You keep writing *he*."

Matt thought for a moment. "That's all right," he said finally. "I think it's grammatically correct to refer to a she as a he until you know she's a she. Of course, once you know he's a she, she can no longer be a he."

Lamar blinked. "Oh . . . okay . . . good. As long as you've thought it out."

Matt found the strange "clock key" just above the "enter" key and pushed it. An animated clock icon flashed on the screen; the one on the screen and the one on the key were the same clock, colored golden, its hands rapidly sweeping forward. That's all it took. Now everything would happen just as Matt typed. He didn't understand how it worked, but it *worked*. Every time Matt hit the clock key, amazing stuff occurred.

Gill reappeared. "The power!" he said, trying to catch his breath.

"The power?"

"The power to the camera's off! I peeked in and the little green light is *off*! It must have a self-powered shutdown!"

Matt's forehead scrunched up. "I thought you said you could control the recording from the AV lab."

"Yes! But the power has to be *on!*"

"Well, go in and turn it on!"

"Right!"

Gill took off.

Gill returned.

"What now?" Matt asked.

"The killer's in there! I just saw the door close! I'm not going in!"

Matt rolled his eyes. "He's not a killer."

"I'm not going in there."

"Well, how are we going to catch him if the camera isn't *on?*"

"Maybe the killer will turn it on."

"The *killer* is not going to turn it on."

"Matt! You've got a cool laptop! Use it!"

Matt huffed, closed the laptop's cover, jumped up, and moved around Gill. "C'mon," he whispered, "I need to see what I'm doing."

The three boys crept up to Coach Plymouth's office, but whoever had gone inside had closed the window blinds. They knelt down and Matt found a pinhole. His heart began to beat wildly as he watched the figure moving around inside Coach's office. Lamar and Gill found their own pinholes and bent around each other to view the action.

"Can you tell who it is?" Gill hissed.

"Not at all," Lamar replied.

Matt hurried back to his laptop. He opened it up and wrote,

> Sure that his diabolical plan to change
> the grades would come to pass, the
> menacing grade-changer sat down at the
> coach's desk, about to check on the
> grades. Suddenly, he spotted a video
> camera across the room.

Matt hit the clock key, then ran back to his pinhole and looked inside. The figure had stopped moving. Matt ran back to his laptop.

> The grade-changer grabbed a football and
> pitched it right at the camera.
>
> Bam! The camera went down, hitting the
> floor fast. As it smashed, the power
> jolted on and it rolled to a spot where
> it put the thief in perfect view.

"What?" Gill cried, looking over Matt's shoulder. "Matt! If that camera busts, I'm in *so much* trouble!"

Matt added:

> The camera didn't bust.

"Thanks."

Matt hit the clock key, ran back to his pinhole, and a moment later, watched as one of Coach's trophies—the one with the big golden football on top—sailed across the room.

Bam! It bounced off the camera and hit the blinds. Matt, Lamar, and Gill jolted back and scattered like birds on a seashore. They darted around the corner as they heard the camera crash to the ground.

Gill peeked around the corner and through the blinds. "Hey, good job, Matt," he whispered. "The camera is right by the window, facing the crook—and powered on."

"Go broadcast that signal!" Matt whispered back.

"Right!"

Gill slinked down the hall and out of sight.

"C'mon," Matt said, tapping Lamar's arm. "Let's go watch in the gym."

He picked up his laptop and threw his blue backpack over his shoulder, then quietly rounded the corner with Lamar and exited the locker room. They crossed the hall to the gym and took seats on the bleachers. They were the only ones there except Coach Plymouth and Alfonzo, who was making baskets from all over the court.

Matt and Lamar stared at the Jumbotron video screen, hovering over the center of the gymnasium.

"C'mon, Gill," Matt mumbled. "C'mon."

Lamar was quiet, his lips moving occasionally.

Nervous, Matt opened up the laptop again.

> One by one, the grade-changer checked the grades. He let out a monster mad scientist laugh, knowing that he was outsmarting the world!
>
> "Muah-ha-ha-ha-ha-ha!"

Pzzzt! Phhatt!

The Jumbotron popped on and Matt knew that all around the school, video feeds were being interrupted as a new video took over. At once, they saw a huge figure, lurking over a computer.

Alfonzo stopped dribbling the basketball and Coach Plymouth's eyebrows furled.

"That . . . that's my office," the coach said slowly. "Who's . . . in there?"

Matt squinted and felt his stomach tighten. He knew the figure . . . he just couldn't make out the face. "Who . . . ?"

Lamar shrugged, squinting.

The gym doors on the far side burst open and Vice-Principal Carter ran in, his tie over his shoulder. "Hey!" he barked at Coach Plymouth. "Isn't that your office?"

Both men squinted at the video feed as the figure tapped on the coach's keyboard.

"Hey! He's using my computer to change grades." Coach realized.

"Who?"

At once, the grade-changer spun around in his chair and laughed like a mad scientist. "Muah-ha-ha-ha-ha-ha!"

Matt felt his body go weak. Yes, he knew that figure. He knew that voice. He knew that face.

It was "Hulk" Hooligan—the biggest, meanest guy in the school.

Matt gulped. "I think it's time to get back to study hall," he said.

Moments later, Matt sat at a table in the library, shaking. Lamar sat beside him. The study hall monitor had just stepped out; he'd heard about a video broadcasting throughout the school, and he wanted to see it for himself.

"What are you afraid of?" Lamar whispered.

"Gill was right," Matt said. "It *was* a killer. And he's going to kill *me!*"

"Matt, he doesn't know you did anything. Look, what he did was wrong. And now he's caught. Remember, you just saved Coach Plymouth's hide."

Matt expelled a long breath. "Yeah, I guess you're right. And that feels pretty good."

"You bet it does!" Lamar agreed.

Bam! Suddenly the library door burst open and Matt jerked back. Standing in the door's frame was Hulk Hooligan—all 250 pounds of him. He glared directly at Matt.

Matt gulped. "He knows."

"He doesn't know," Lamar whispered, not moving his lips. "He *can't* know. Keep your cool."

Hulk stomped into the room like a T-Rex, causing nearby bookshelves to shake. A bead of perspiration trickled down the back of Matt's neck.

As Hulk crossed the room, Matt heard some girls whispering about the video, which didn't help at all. Hulk stopped on the other side of Matt and Lamar's table and glared at Matt.

"Hey, Hulk," Lamar greeted him.

"Do ya' know what jus' happened to me?" he asked Matt through gritted teeth.

Matt quickly shook his head. "I . . . uh . . ."

"I was jus' told I could be *expelled*, Calhan," Hulk announced.

His words hung in the air.

"C-c-cal-*a*-han," Matt said, choking on his last name.

"Don't know how," he blustered, "but dey found out I hacked Coach's computer and changed my

English grade to an A. Pretty smart, eh? I had even covered my tracks by changing some of da other kids' grades. But somehow dey found out."

Suddenly the library door burst open and Gill ran in, his head bouncing. "I did it!" he shouted, "I—"

Then he spotted Hulk. "I—" Gill threw a finger up in the air. "I . . . have to go to the bathroom. Excuse me!" And he ran back out the door.

Hulk shook his head. "Dat kid's strange," he said.

"Heh-heh," Matt chuckled. Then, "Hulk, I'm sorry, but—"

"Good!" Hulk shouted, slamming his fists on the table.

Matt and Lamar jumped.

"I'm *glad* you're sorry, 'cuz you're gonna help me!"

"I . . . I am?"

"Yeah, ya are. See, I've been given one week to pass last week's English exam."

"*Last* week's English exam?"

"Yeah—dey want me to retake it. I have t' pass or I'm out of here. Ya wouldn't want dat now, would ya?"

Matt thought about that for a moment.

Hulk slammed his fist on the table.

"No, no, I wouldn't want that."

"I didn't think so."

"So . . . what do you want me to do?"

"Well, I always see ya typin' on yer laptop, and I know yer good at English. Ya jus' became my tutor."

"Your *tutor?*"

Hulk reached across the table and grabbed Matt by the collar. Matt popped up out of his chair and leaned over the table as Hulk pulled Matt's face close to his own.

"Ya have a *problem* with dat?"

Matt winced at Hulk's breath.

"We start tomorrow, after school, at my locker."

"Right," Matt squeaked.

Hulk pushed Matt back and let go. Matt crumbled into his seat. Hulk spun around and started walking away.

"Uh, Hulk?"

The mammoth bully stopped. He didn't turn around. "What?"

"What . . . um . . . what happens if we do all this studying and . . . and you don't pass?"

Hulk cracked his knuckles and snickered. "Use your imagination."

2

The Ultimate Test

'm dead. Just dead. Start planning my funeral."

Matt was eyeing his neck in the mirror, noting that it was still slightly red from where Hulk had grabbed him.

The four boys—the QoolQuad, as Matt called them—were together as usual. Lamar lay on Matt's bed, sketching in a notepad, while Gill flipped through an old *TV Guide*. Alfonzo, Matt's new neighbor from across the street, rolled a faded basketball around in his hands.

Matt shook his head. "You know my social life has ended."

"You don't have a social life," Gill stated flatly, not looking up.

Matt turned around. "Thanks, Gill."

Gill motioned toward Matt's laptop, sitting on the pine desk under his window. "Why don't you just use the laptop to help Hulk pass the test?"

"That gets my vote," Matt offered.

"Oh, that's good," Lamar quickly interjected. "Hulk gets in trouble for fixing grades, and you want to get him out of trouble by fixing his grade."

Matt took a deep breath. "Well, we said we wanted to use the laptop to make dreams come true. How about my dream to live?"

"How about your dream to follow our honor code and do what's right?"

"I know. I know."

Gill closed the *TV Guide*. "Hey, speaking of which. How about making my dream come true? Make my audition for this commercial go great."

"You really gonna audition?" Lamar asked.

Gill nodded. "Yeah. And if you're nice to me, I'll get you a Lamborghini when I'm famous."

"I'd rather have a Porsche," Lamar noted.

"But back to the subject at hand . . ." Matt said loudly. "What am I supposed to do? I have to tutor Hulk for a *week*. It's an impossible venture."

"Hulk's a bully because that's all he knows," Lamar offered. "I'm sure there's more to him than we can imagine. He just never lets anyone in."

"I don't think there's anything more to Hulk," Matt noted. "He's just a bully and does whatever he wants to get his way. I've known him for *five years*. He's a bully through and through. Maybe his school problems have made him into a bully, but there's not much I can do about that."

The boys sat silent for a long moment. Alfonzo stopped rolling the basketball around and finally spoke up. "It could be a good challenge." Everyone looked at Alfonzo, a little surprised he'd said anything. He'd become a regular part of the group by now, always up for sports and fun. But when they talked, he was usually quiet.

"What could be a good challenge?" Matt asked.

"Using the laptop to fix Hulk's problems. You were able to make Mr. Gillespie's dream come true. You were able to get Coach Plymouth out of a hard place. Why not use the laptop to try to solve Hulk's problems?"

"You think I *should* use the laptop to make him smart? Change his grade?" Matt scratched his head. "I don't know . . ."

"No. I mean use it to help him learn. Use it to make him nice."

"Impossible."

"You know, that's not a bad idea," Lamar said. "Why not see what the laptop can do? Besides, you know, when God gives you a gift, you gotta use it."

Matt sat down at his desk chair and ran his right hand over the laptop's black plastic case. "God knows that I need help tutoring him. I guess it's worth a shot."

"Yeah," Lamar said. "Remember the 2:52 thing Pastor Ruhlen taught us? The Bible says when Jesus was our age, he grew in wisdom and stature, and in favor with God and men. Well, just like Jesus, we're all growing—and your strength is your wisdom. Use your smarts with the laptop and you can teach Hulk a thing or two."

Matt nodded. Maybe Lamar was right. Maybe he really could help Hulk. It was worth a shot.

Suddenly Gill clapped his hands.

Everyone jumped.

"Hey," he said, laughing. "Speaking of smarts, I had an idea the other night."

"All things are possible," Matt jested.

"Ha-ha. Seriously, I may have a way we can track down more information about your laptop."

"Yeah, how?" Matt asked.

"Well," Gill began, "when we got you your Web site—QoolQuad.com—we had to register it on the Internet."

"Yeah . . ."

"Well . . . *anyone* can see that registration. They just go to the Internet registry service and you're listed as the one who registered it."

"Right. Just like the phone book."

"Exactly!" Gill declared. "So if we go to the registry service and type in Wordtronix.com—the website of the laptop company—maybe we can find out re about who owns the company and where they're located."

Matt's eyebrows shot up.

Lamar's eyebrows shot up.

Alfonzo's eyebrows shot up.

"Good idea, eh?" Gill's ears wiggled under his red hair.

Matt swung around and popped open the laptop's lid. He booted up and logged onto the Internet as fast as he could. Lamar, Gill, and Alfonzo gathered around him, leaning into the glowing laptop screen.

Matt brought up the Web browser and typed in the address to the registry service. When the page appeared, he located the search box and typed, "WORDTRONIX.COM." An icon twirled on the browser and the results lit up the screen:

```
www.wordtronix.com
Registrant: Wordtronix (WORDTRONIX.COM)
123 Main Street
City, US 12345
Domain Name: WORDTRONIX.COM
Administrative Contact, Billing Contact:
Wordtronix administrator@WORDTRONIX.COM
123 Main Street
City, US 12345
Technical Contact:
Administrator, DNS
administrator@WORDTRONIX.COM
Record created on 24-Sep-1999.
```

The boys studied it for a long moment before saying anything. Finally, Alfonzo said, "US? What state is that?"

Matt shook his head. "It's not a state. And look at this address: 123 Main Street. This is all bogus."

"Well, I'm not surprised," Lamar admitted.

Matt opened his mouth to say something else when—

"Hi, guys!"

Matt slammed the laptop shut and all four boys spun around to see Alfonzo's twelve-year-old sister, Isabel, standing in Matt's doorway. Matt suddenly lost his breath and his mouth went dry. Isabel's straight black hair tumbled around her shoulders, cradling her cheeks. Her deep brown eyes were wide. She was surely wondering what she had just interrupted.

"Hola, Iz," Alfonzo greeted in his native Spanish.

Isabel entered the room, taking each step carefully. "Hola. Hi, Lamar, Gill"—she looked right at Matt—"Matt."

He waved sheepishly, wondering if his neck was still red.

"What you guys doing?"

Lamar said, "Surfing."

Gill said, "Playing."

Alfonzo said, "Writing."

Matt said, "Pthhh."

Isabel popped her lips. "Okay . . ."

The four boys stared at the intruder. Finally, she said something in Spanish to Alfonzo.

"My dad has dinner ready," he told them. "I have to go."

They all nodded.

Isabel added, "Matt, your mama told me to tell you that your dinner's ready, too."

Matt was speechless, struck with how much her words sounded like newly spun honey. Lamar nudged him in the ribs and, jolted, he said, "Tanks! I afishitate two yelling me!"

Isabel giggled and grabbed her brother's hand, pulling him away from the group. Alfonzo tucked his basketball under his arm, and they exited the room.

Lamar and Gill stepped back on either side of Matt and said, "*I afishitate two yelling me?*"

Matt threw his hands up. "What?"

Mr. Calahan walked in from the garage and kissed his wife on the cheek. He apologized for being ten minutes late, explaining that he had some kind of work emergency from which he couldn't get away. Mrs. Calahan said it was all right and pointed at the dishes on the table—she had prepared a salad and lasagna. Matt and his mom had already finished their salads, but knowing his dad's appetite, Matt figured he'd catch up soon.

Penny Calahan pushed her chair back and walked over to the counter. She returned with a small folded flyer, which she set down beside her husband. He read it and said, "You want to go to this, Matt?"

Matt stopped chewing his cheesy lasagna. "Go to what?"

Stan Calahan slid the flyer down the table and positioned it in front of Matt. It was the Enisburg Community Church bulletin. Matt usually didn't read the church bulletin because it was all announcements for adults about baby showers, prayer services, and potluck dinners.

Circled in red ink at the bottom of the second fold was the announcement:

2:52 Youth Group Father-Son Retreat
Join us November 18–21 for a super-colossal time in the Lord!

"Super-colossal." It had to be written by the church's new youth pastor, Mick Ruhlen. Matt liked him, but he was something else. It continued.

We'll be "roughing it" for a weekend of fun— camping, playing sports, talking, and seeking the Lord near Landes, Arizona. Register today and be a part of the bash!

Matt wiped his mouth with his napkin. "I don't know . . ." He could already envision it. He wouldn't be able to shower for four days. Two thousand mosquitoes would attack him. The food would be so bad he wouldn't be able to distinguish the chicken from the potatoes. The dads would get all caught up in talking about their careers. And there wouldn't be an Internet connection for miles. Why would *anyone* want to go to a camp like that? Besides, as usual, just when he and his dad would start talking, Mr. Calahan would be interrupted by a call from work he "had" to take. Matt could already feel himself getting frustrated.

> "Speaking of friends, I just met Isabel Zarza from across the street. She's a cutie."

"Well," Matt's dad said, "let me know if you want to go. This is a busy time of year, but I might be able to find a way if we plan far enough in advance." He scratched his head.

Matt smiled and nodded. Maybe his dad would forget about it.

"So what happened to you today, Matt?" his dad asked, changing the subject.

Matt rubbed his neck. "Same ol', same ol'. I'm going to be tutoring Hulk Hooligan in English all next week. He needs help."

Mrs. Calahan stopped eating. "You mean that big boy who always knocked you down in football practice?"

"That would be him."

"Oh, my. I didn't realize you two were friends."

"Well, we're more study partners than friends."

Mrs. Calahan cleared her throat. "Speaking of friends, I just met Isabel Zarza from across the street. She's a cutie."

Matt about choked. Okay, now it really *was* time to change the subject.

"That's Alfonzo's sister, right?" Mr. Calahan asked. "Yeah, I like them both. I still need to talk to their father about a construction job in his basement."

"So how was your guys' day?" Mrs. Calahan asked.

Mr. Calahan took a sip of iced tea and then leaned back. "Well, I wish *I* could say it was same ol', same ol'."

"What happened?" Mrs. Calahan asked.

"Well, you remember all the trouble I've been having with Harry?"

"Mmm-hmm."

"Well, I couldn't figure out why he'd been slacking off lately. You know, Harry's a guy I've always been able to count on." Mr. Calahan turned to Matt. "Harry's the best electrician in Enisburg. But lately, he's been goofing up more than he's been showing up."

"So what was wrong?" Mrs. Calahan stood up and moved the baked lasagna to the kitchen counter for wrapping.

"Well, Harry's messed up real bad, Penny." Matt's dad glanced at him. "There's no need to go into it, but I found out this morning that Harry has no place to stay this whole week. His life has been turned upside down."

Mrs. Calahan stopped spreading foil over the lasagna dish and turned around. "Oh, my. What'd you do?"

"Fortunately, I was able to pull a few favors and get him put up for the next week at Gardener's Hotel. I'm giving him an advance on his next few jobs to help him out. It's about all I can do right now, but every bit helps."

Matt's mom walked over and slid her arms around her husband's neck. She kissed him on the top of his head. "You just performed a miracle in that man's life," she said. "You're so compassionate."

"I'm just solving the problem," he responded.

"Sometimes," Mrs. Calahan interjected, "that's exactly what compassion is."

The post-dinner blues hit Matt between the eyes like one of the footballs he had intercepted last season. He reclined on the couch in the living room, not wanting to move a muscle. Some nature program about spiders was on *Animal Planet*. It wasn't nearly as exciting as the crocodile guy.

All Matt could think about was the fact that tomorrow he would start tutoring the one enemy he'd made in junior high. For the entire next week, he was stuck with Hulk—unless of course he opted for his own death sentence, no thank you. Maybe Gill was right and he could use the laptop for an edge, but . . . this was almost impossible. Solve Hulk's problems? Make him an English genius? Hulk could barely speak English correctly, let alone write the great American essay.

Matt let out a long breath and changed the channel. On FOX, he found a special called *Amazing Stunts 4*. As if anyone ever watched *Amazing Stunts 1, 2,* or *3*. A helicopter was cutting through the air, a man dangling from a long cord, doing acrobats. "Check out that aerial artistry!" the announcer said. "You don't see this caliber of daredevil dynamics anywhere else in the world!"

Just going up in a helicopter makes you a daredevil, Matt thought. Those things were scary. Maybe he'd seen too many movies where they went plummeting into the ground or crashed into skyscrapers.

Matt punched the power button on the remote control. He picked himself up off the couch and trudged upstairs. Maybe he was making too big a deal of it all. Maybe it was just the gooey cheese from dinner making him tired. Then again, maybe it was because he had looked like a fool in front of his whole school when Hulk threatened him in study hall.

When Matt entered his room, he noticed Lamar's sketch pad still on his bed. He plopped down on the edge of his bed and flipped it open. Lamar had drawn several QoolQuad logos for their Web site. Matt knew he had to get to work on their site—and fast—if they were going to have anything out there for the world to see.

He turned the page—Superman, bulging with muscles. Lamar had drawn him with dark skin, which Matt thought looked pretty cool. Then he realized the "S" on the character's chest was actually an "L" and his face favored Lamar. Matt chuckled.

Page 3 was empty of drawings. A lone Bible verse stared back at him:

Luke 15:20

Leave it to Lamar to give Matt a hint. He pulled his Bible off his nightstand and found the verse. "But while he was still a long way off, his father saw him and was filled with compassion for him."

It was a verse in the story of the Prodigal Son— the story about the boy who took his inheritance, left his father, blew his inheritance, and then returned. But instead of being mad at his son, the father had compassion on him and accepted him back.

Matt knew he had to be compassionate with Hulk. It just wasn't easy. Hulk was *such* a long way off from where he needed to be. He was *such* the typical bully.

Matt changed into a pair of shorts and a T-shirt. Raindrops began hitting his window.

Perhaps God was giving him an opportunity to be a light to Hulk. Perhaps this was all part of God's plan to solve Hulk's problems and show him exactly what God could do—and what Hulk could do if he set his mind to it. Perhaps everything was about to change.

Or, then again, maybe it was just going to be a bad week.

Rain, Rain, Go Away

3

*D*ay One

Like the weather outside, Matt felt completely dreary. He was headed out the front of the school when Hulk blindsided him from the right and pushed him up against the wall.

"Where ya goin'?" he demanded.

Overtaken with surprise, Matt stuttered, "T-t-to your house."

"How d'ya know where I live?"

"I looked it up on the Internet and printed out a map." Matt held up the map for Hulk to see.

Hulk grabbed it and crumpled it up with one hand. "We're not goin' to my house, Calhan."

"Cal-*a*-han."

"Whatever. We're stayin' here. We'll meet in da lunchroom. Every day. Got it?"

Matt huffed. "Got it." It was going to be a *long* week.

Hulk let go, turned around, and walked toward the lunchroom. Matt shifted his backpack so that it was balanced once again and followed.

The lunchroom was empty save for two giggling eighth grade girls on the other side of the room. Hulk picked a nearby table and thumped down on a bench. The table shook. Matt took a seat on the opposite side. Both boys looked at each other.

"So what do I have to teach you?" Matt said finally.

Hulk grunted, "English," as if Matt were stupid.

"Can you be more specific?"

"No."

"Do you have a book?"

"It's in my locker."

"I think we'll need it."

"K."

"Do you want to get it?"

"No."

Matt tightened his lips. Yes, one *long, long* week.

Matt pulled out his own English book and cracked it open to chapter two. He set it on the table and turned it around so Hulk could see it. But Hulk was busy glaring at the girls.

"Here are some grammar exercises," Matt pointed out. "Why don't we take them one by one."

Hulk didn't respond.

Matt read the first one. "In the sentence, 'The shiny trophy glistened in the light,' what is the word *shiny*? A noun? A verb? Adjective? Adv—"

"Baaaaarrrrrraaaaappppp!" belched Hulk.

Matt's face contorted. The two girls shot them an irritated look.

Matt tried not to get flustered. He waited for an answer. "Well . . ."

"Barrapp! Barrapp!" belched Hulk. The girls hopped up and left.

Matt scratched his head. "Okay, you're close, but the answer was 'an adjective.' Let's go back and start with something a little less . . . challenging . . ." He turned the pages back and found another question.

 "In the sentence, 'My dog loves to chew on a bone,' is the word *bone* a noun or a verb?"

Hulk sat still for a moment and then slid his left arm under his shirt. He lifted his right arm and then squeezed it down against his side. A loud "phhhhhhaaattt!" exploded into the room. He guffawed. "Haw! Haw! Haw! Bet you can't do that, Calhan! Haw! Haw!"

Yep, a very *long* week.

Day Two

"All right," Matt said, sitting down across from Hulk for the second time. "Yesterday we got nowhere, but today we're going to study. I'm going to teach and you're going to answer—with *words*. No bodily functions. No unusual noises. Nothing that requires air freshener. I've only got one week to teach you this or you said you'd kill me, and I'm not ready to die, you got it?"

Matt felt the beads of perspiration gathering on his upper lip. Hulk shifted his gaze to Matt and his lips turned up in a smirk. "I never knew ya had it in ya, Calhan."

"Me neither. And it's Cal-*a*-han," Matt corrected, thanking God for his laptop. Fifteen minutes prior, he had typed:

> When the handsome tutor, Matt Calahan,
> laid it on the line with his nemesis,
> Hulk Hooligan, Hulk's anger subsided and
> he agreed to cooperate. And Hulk brought
> his own English book.

Matt smiled. "Okay. Forget nouns and adjectives. Let's move to euphemisms. You have your book?"

Hulk pulled it out and placed it on the table.

"Page 46." They both turned there. "Okay, the first one. What's a euphemism for 'visually impaired'?"

Hulk stared at the page for a full thirty seconds and moved his lips as he read. "Okay, what's a euphemism?" he asked finally.

"Well, we talked about it last week in class. Right before the test. It's a nice way of saying something that may seem unpleasant. It's like being politically correct."

Hulk's eyes glazed over.

"So 'visually impaired' is a nice way of saying 'blind.'"

Hulk's lips parted slightly.

"Or," Matt said, breaking it down, "'mentally impaired' is a euphemism for 'stupid.'"

Hulk's eyes narrowed.

"No!" Matt cried. "I'm not implying anything . . . just an example."

Hulk let out a breath.

"So, what is 'economically disadvantaged' a euphemism for?"

Hulk thought for another fifteen seconds. "Poor?"

Matt's mouth dropped open. "That's . . . that's *right.*"

Hulk smiled. "I'm brilliant."

"Tell me what 'involuntary servitude' is a euphemism for . . ."

"Um . . . slavery?"

"Right! Good! Let's turn it the other way around. Give me a euphemism for 'out of work.'"

Hulk paused for several moments, then, "Between jobs?"

"Yes!" Matt wanted to jump out of his seat and do the Macarena on the table. "Now give me a euphemism for 'dead.'"

Hulk looked down at the table and thought for a long moment, then mumbled, "I don't think dere's any nice way to say dat."

Day Three

"Vocabulary," Matt stated.

"Can I burp today?"

"No. But you *can* give me definitions. First word: *secluded*. What's it mean?"

Hulk twisted his lip.

"Have you been paying attention in class?" Matt asked, sounding like his mom.

"Yeah," Hulk said, sounding put out.

"Well?"

"I think we should start with another word."

"You want to know what it means?"

"Next word, Calhan!"

"Okay. How about *appall*."

Hulk leaned back. "Oh, I got dat. Dat's whatchu put a flag on, right?"

Matt shook his head. "Funny. Let's try another: *assent*."

"Four pennies less den a nickel."

"I'm tutoring a comedian. How about *demur*."

"Da mother of a calf."

"I think I preferred the belching."

Day Four

"I don't understand why you don't just use the laptop to make him smarter," Gill pressed, passing the basketball to Matt as they jogged across the gym. It was still raining like cats and dogs, way too wet for playing on the outside courts.

"I *am* using the laptop." Matt dribbled the ball twice, then passed it to Lamar. "Every day I write in it that he'll be nice, concentrate, and not be a dimwit. I don't know. Sometimes it works, sometimes it doesn't. I don't know why. And then sometimes it backfires."

"Backfires?"

"How do you think I got this bruise on my arm?"

"What happened?" Lamar asked, passing the ball to Alfonzo.

"I'm the Slammer!" Alfonzo shouted as he shot a three-pointer.

Matt recovered the ball and then held it as he spoke. "Today I tutored Hulk in poetry. It's not as easy as it sounds. I told him he had to make stuff rhyme. He looks at me completely blank, so I say, 'Well, what rhymes with *tree*?'"

"And he says . . ."

"Leaf."

Lamar, Gill, and Alfonzo all winced.

"Yeah, so I said, okay, forget the rhyming. We'll write haikus. All you have to do is write five syllables, followed by seven syllables, followed by five syllables. And I gave him an example I wrote earlier."

> *The rain fell softly*
> *As God's tears for fallen man.*
> *The Son stopped the rain.*

"Man, that's good," Lamar complimented.

"Thanks." Matt turned to Gill. "Then I used the laptop."

> Hulk writes a haiku that moves me to tears.

"I thought, *How can I go wrong?* Right?"

"Right."

"So he writes his haiku and then slips me the paper."

> *Food is good for you.*
> *Potatoes taste good with cheese.*
> *Boogers are salty.*

Lamar, Gill, and Alfonzo were on the floor laughing. "Yeah, that's what I did, too," Matt said. "I laughed so hard, I cried. The laptop worked all right.

And Hulk punched me in the arm. And you know what the worst thing is? It's actually a good haiku!"

Day Five

"So when you write a story," Matt was saying, "one of the basic rules is 'Show, don't tell.'"

"I don't get it," Hulk said.

"Let me explain. It means that instead of just saying something flat out, you show the reader what you want them to see."

"I don't get it."

"Okay, for instance, instead of just coming out and saying, 'Fred is sad,' you say, 'Fred's gut was tight as his bottom lip protruded out.' See, you're saying he's sad without actually *saying* he's sad."

"Why not jus' come out and say it?"

"Because . . . it's more literary not to."

"I don't get it."

"Well, you see, it's better to give the reader a picture than to tell them flat out what's happening."

"Who's Fred anyway?"

"Okay, I think that concludes today's lesson."

Day Six

"E-M-E-R-G-E-N-C-Y."

"That's right!" Matt shouted. "Good! Spelling must be your strong point! I knew you'd have one! Okay, let's try another word: *debt*."

"D-E-T."

"Close. It's D-E-*B*-T. How about *automobile?*"

"C-A-R."

"He's a comedian again. C'mon. For real. *Automobile*."

"A-U-T-A-M-O-B-I-L-E."

"No, it's A-U-T-*O*-M-O-B-I-L-E. How about *billion?*"

"B-I-L-I-O-N."

"Close again, but two L's. Now *debt*."

"D-E-T."

Matt studied Hulk's face for a moment and then asked, "How is it that you can spell a hard word like *emergency*, but not *debt, automobile,* or *billion?*"

Hulk shrugged.

Day Seven

On the final day of tutoring, Matt rehashed grammar, euphemisms, vocabulary, spelling, poetry, and story-telling techniques. He was actually surprised at how well Hulk was coming along. He knew there was probably no way the big guy would ever pass his test (which meant by tomorrow at this time Matt would be six feet under the ground), but all things considered, he was doing a lot better than Matt had anticipated.

At the end of the day, Matt gave Hulk a word or two of encouragement, then added, "You're going to have to write a short essay, too. Just don't sweat it. Write what you know and you'll do fine. They're not as interested in grammar and spelling and stuff on your essay. They just want to see that you can put your thoughts on paper. All right?"

Hulk nodded.

Matt waited for him to say thanks, but he didn't.

"I'm gonna pass this," Hulk finally muttered.

"I believe you will," Matt said hopefully.

"Well, don't expect me to come runnin' to ya when I do. It's no big deal."

"Just letting me live is payment enough."

"See ya 'round, Calhan," Hulk said, turning to leave.

"I'll be praying for you," Matt promised as Hulk walked away. *Man, you're going to need it . . .*

4

Testing Results

The wet weather gave Southern California a break for the afternoon, and it felt great to be outside. The air was fresh with the sweet smell of rain. After school, Matt found himself at home alone, wearing a well-paced circle in his bedroom carpet. Earlier that day, he had been tempted to type, "Hulk aces his English test," into the laptop, but fought against it. Lamar was right—it would be the same as fixing Hulk's grade.

Matt looked at his watch. By now, the test was over. He wasn't sure why he cared so much that Hulk passed. But he did. Feeling fidgety and impatient, Matt scrawled a note to his mom on a Post-It that he'd be over at a friend's house. Then he screamed out of the garage on his bike.

According to his newly printed map, Hulk's house was 3.2 miles away from Matt's, but with shortcuts through a few parking lots, it seemed to go a lot faster. Like a skier in the winter Olympics, he dodged about fifty thousand puddles and finally came to a screeching halt in front of a sign: "Park Glen."

Matt double-checked his map again. Yep, this was it. He hopped off his bicycle and walked into the sub-division, looking for 1791 Wellington Court. The homes here looked weathered from time, like they were built long before the homes in Matt's neck of the woods. The flower boxes were mostly empty and the lawns were more weeds than grass. Several people were outside, sitting on their porches or standing on the sidewalk talking to one another. One little girl, clad only in a diaper, was running away from her mother. Matt chuckled. Finally, he found Wellington Court. He turned the corner and Hulk's house was the second one he came to. The gray house looked as if it had been dropped on the lot without any care for exact placement. Like Matt's own home, it was built from wood. It almost appeared unlived-in, but Matt spotted fresh oil on the driveway. Rainwater made the entire house glisten, like the inside of a bathtub after a shower.

Matt set his bike against a large rock and made his way to the front door. He hopped up the cement steps, knocked lightly on the screen door, and waited. He knocked again. Apparently, Hulk wasn't home yet. Oh well, it had been a nice ride over.

Matt returned to his bike and picked it up. He threw a leg over the body frame, looked up at the house once more, and then—wait, what was that? The drapery waved as if someone was just there. Matt stared at it for a short time, but it stopped moving.

Slowly, Matt put his bike back down. He kept his eyes on the window as he stepped across the cracking driveway. He drew closer so that he could see the dirt streak trails from yesterday's shower . . .

Matt positioned himself directly underneath the window and then slowly rose up. He peered over the bottom pane, squinting to see if he could make out anything inside. Maybe a cat, maybe a dog, maybe a—

BAM! Suddenly a head popped up in front of Matt's!

"Aaaaaagggghhhhhh!" Matt cried, stumbling back.

Matt's heart pounded as he stared at the vacant window. Slowly the head appeared again.

"Aaaaaagggghhhhhh!" the head cried, then disappeared.

Matt's heart pounded as he stared at the vacant window. Slowly the head appeared again. It was a perfectly round face—a boy who couldn't be more than seven years old. Bright blue eyes and rosy cheeks framed themselves in the window. A tuft of blond hair stuck straight up off the top of his head.

Something was oddly familiar about the boy ... yeah, he looked just like Hulk—but about seven years younger ... and 150 pounds lighter.

Cautiously, Matt waved.

The boy waved back.

Matt smiled.

The boy smiled.

Matt's heart returned to a normal beat. He pointed to the door and the boy disappeared. A moment later, the main door swung open and the boy stood there, parading his red fire engine pajamas.

"Hi," Matt greeted, through the screen door. "Is Hulk home?"

The boy shook his head.

"Does Hulk live here?"

The boy nodded.

"Do you call him Hulk?"

"I call 'im Bo-bo head."

Matt laughed. Yep, he was in the right place.

"Do you know when he's getting home?"

"No. I like pizza."

"You do? Me too. Well, will you tell him Matt stopped by?"

"My name is Nathaniel David Hooligan, but they call me Nate."

"My name is Matthew Roberts Calahan, but they call me Matt."

"That's a funny name." Then Nate let out a burp and giggled.

Matt's raised his eyebrows. "It runs in the family, I see."

"What are *you* doin' here?" an unmistakable voice boomed from behind.

Matt twirled around to see Hulk approaching fast.

"I–I–I came to see how you did on your test," Matt blurted.

"I did fine," Hulk blustered, then to Nate, "What're ya doin' up? Where's Dad?"

Nate shrugged. "I like pizza."

"I know ya do. Get back in your bedroom."

Nate swung around and ran off.

"What'd he tell ya?" Hulk demanded.

> Matt walked past Hulk. "I don't care where you live," he mumbled, "I just came to see how you did."

"Nothing. Just that he liked pizza, but that's apparently common knowledge."

"I didn't tell ya that ya could come here."

"I just came to see how you did on the test."

"I did fine. A seventy. I passed."

"You did? That's great!"

"Fine. Ya can go now."

"All right," Matt conceded. What had he expected? Matt walked past Hulk. "I don't care where you live," he mumbled, "I just came to see how you did."

"Hey!"

"What?" Matt shouted back, whirling around.

"I ain't ashamed of where I live. You're so . . . Just 'cuz ya got a perfect life don't mean ya can judge the way I live!"

"I don't have a perfect life and I'm not judging the way you live! I just came to see how you did!"

"I did fine!"

"Fine!" Matt repeated, spotting movement behind Hulk.

"What?" Hulk asked, gaping at Matt.

Matt pointed. "Your little brother's in the doorway again."

Hulk turned around. "Get in bed!"

Nate giggled and ran off.

"I didn't know you had a brother," Matt said. "Guess he beat you home from school."

Hulk huffed. "He don't go to school, Calhan."

"Cal-*a*-han. Why not? Does your grandmother home school him?"

"My gramma don't live here."

"Oh—I thought she did since she brings you to church. Who do you live with?"

"Harm."

"Harm?"

"My dad."

"Your dad's name is Harm?"

"He's not much of a dad. Anything else?"

"No . . . I . . . just wanted to see how you did on your test."

"I did fine. Ya solved all my problems."

"Right." Matt didn't want to push, but the investigative reporter in him was starting to come out. After being in school with Godzilla for five years, it seemed a bit strange that he never even knew he had a brother.

"So your dad must home school him, huh?"

Hulk grunted. "He don't go to school right now. He's waitin' for surgery."

Matt blinked. That hit him out of left field. "For . . . what?"

Hulk shifted his weight impatiently. He looked back at the empty

> Hulk shifted his weight impatiently. "He's waitin' for a new heart," he said in a hushed tone.

doorway, then back at Matt. "He's waitin' for a new heart," he said in a hushed tone. "He's next on the list, but it takes a while. He has to stay in bed 'cuz he ain't doin' so good."

Matt opened his mouth, but nothing came out.

"He ain't dyin'," Hulk added quickly. "He's just . . . not doin' well, okay?" He sniffed. "So dat's it. Ya know everything. Ya can leave now. But if ya tell anyone, you're dead. I'm only tellin' ya 'cuz ya helped me on this test."

"I'm . . . sorry . . ." Matt said slowly, looking at the doorway.

"Don't be. Go home to yer white picket fence and forget about it. There's nothin' ya can do."

"We, uh . . . don't have a white picket fence."

"It's a euphemism, Calhan."

"Oh . . . right."

Hulk turned and stomped into his house, letting the screen door slam behind him.

Matt picked up his bicycle and looked up at the window once more. Nate's bright blue eyes stared back at him. Matt took a deep breath and mounted his bike. As he moved down the sidewalk and out into the street, he realized he didn't know Hulk nearly as well as he thought he did. In fact, he now had the feeling that passing an English test was the *least* of Hulk's problems.

5

Hospital Rush

The word *tense* could only begin to explain the entire next week. Matt had told Lamar, Gill, and Alfonzo, about Hulk's little brother, and they decided they would pray for him. Matt even wrote a short paragraph in the laptop to ensure Nate's well-being. It said:

> Nate Hooligan, a real fighter, had a heart that became healthier than ever and beat strong and well. His sudden recovery amazed friends and family. Soon he was learning, playing with other kids, and getting ready to change the world!

Still, they hadn't received word that Nate was doing any better, and none of them knew quite how to act around Hulk. The big lug was being his usual troublemaker self, which made being around him a trial and a half. Matt and Lamar had tried talking to him, but he left in a huff when he found out Matt had shared his secret. Gill had tried telling him some jokes, but Hulk didn't get them. The closest any of them got to real conversation was when Alfonzo talked to him for a while about football. But even that was pretty tense.

Matt, Lamar, and Alfonzo were in P.E. class practicing their free throws when Gill burst through the gym door pushing a TV and VCR cart in front of him.

Coach Plymouth blew his whistle twice. "Here's the video!" he announced.

The students gathered and sat on the bleachers. Gill positioned the TV so everyone could see. After Coach explained that it was about basketball technique, he pushed "Play."

Gill hopped up to the fourth row of the bleachers and sat behind Matt, Lamar, and Alfonzo. "Guys," he whispered, "I was just setting up in Ms. Henderson's history class and while I was there, Hulk's dad came to get him. Something's up with his little brother. I heard his dad mention the hospital."

"The hospital?" Lamar repeated. "Matt, didn't you write about Nate in your laptop?"

"Yeah ... I don't get it." Matt bit his lip and glanced up at the caged gym clock. "We still have an hour and a half of school left. You guys wanna go there after we get out?"

"You mean to the hospital?"

"Yeah."

They all nodded.

"Hewwo!" exclaimed the man on the TV screen. He was a tall Caucasian, in his early twenties, wearing bright purple shorts and a tank top. "My name is Ewwin Woyce—but you pwobably know me as the Slammew!"

Matt about burst out laughing. "What did he just say?" he whispered.

"That's the Slammer," Alfonzo pointed out, slapping Matt's knee. "He's the best basketball player ever."

"You haven't heard of the Slammer?" Lamar asked.

"I've never heard of him," Gill said, "but he *must* be cool. Check it out—he's a redhead!"

"Well, I've *heard* of him," Matt answered, "but I've never *seen* him. He talks like that?"

"You won't care how he talks when you see him play," Alfonzo stated. "I want to be that good some day."

"He sounds like Elmer Fudd!" Matt said.

"Well, he doesn't play like Elmer Fudd," Alfonzo replied.

The Enisburg Central Hospital smelled like a cross between blue glass cleaner and cherry sore throat spray. The walls and tiled floor were all white and smooth, like the city pool when they remove the water for cleaning. Mr. Calahan, running between business errands, was able to pick the QoolQuad up from school and take them to the hospital. He accompanied them through the automatic sliding glass doors and helped them find the exact location of Nathaniel Hooligan's room. As they walked down the hall, they passed a blue arrow: "EMERGENCY ROOM." So that explained why Hulk could spell *emergency*.

They made their way into Nate's room, but they weren't quite prepared for what they saw. Nate lay on a hospital bed, a single white sheet tucked loosely around his body. A thin, clear tube was wrapped around his head, running under his nose. Several machines blipped and beeped, giving comfort that he was still under the doctor's control. Nate was fast asleep—or unconscious—Matt wasn't sure. His breathing seemed uneven and his skin seemed slightly blue as though he were lying under a party light.

Hulk's grandmother sat quietly by the bed holding Nate's hand. On the other side of the room, Hulk slumped in a corner chair. And a man—Hulk's dad?—paced back and forth nervously.

> They weren't quite prepared for what they saw. Nate lay on a hospital bed, a single white sheet tucked loosely around his body.

It took only a moment for Hulk to see them enter the room. He looked at his dad, then pushed himself up quickly and stopped them in their tracks.

"What're ya doin' here, Calhan?" he said, just above a whisper.

"We heard Nate was here."

"We don't want to disturb your family," Matt's dad added. "We just wanted to stop by and pray."

Hulk fidgeted and then looked back at his brother. "Yeah, okay," he said finally as he stepped aside. "He's been slipping in and out of consciousness. Doc says he needs a heart soon."

Harm Hooligan stopped pacing. He was a short, thin man, ironically the opposite of Hulk, who was tall and wide. He had dark skin, as if he worked outside, and sandy brown hair. His face was worn as if he had seen too many years of trouble. He pulled Hulk to the side. "Who are they?" he demanded.

"Dey're from my school. Dey came to pray for Nate."

Mr. Hooligan rolled his dark eyes and then walked past them without a glance. A few seconds later, he was out of the room.

Hulk was noticeably embarrassed, angry, and downcast all at once. "You know my gramma," he said, angling his head toward the woman positioned by the bed. She looked up and smiled at them slightly. Hulk returned to his corner chair.

Mr. Calahan's cellular phone rang. He pulled it off his belt, looked at the display, then dismissed himself. Lamar looked at Matt, but Matt focused on Nate.

Matt, Lamar, Gill, and Alfonzo approached the side of the boy's bed. It was the first time Lamar, Gill, and Alfonzo had seen Nate. Matt had seen him only a week ago, popping in and out of a window frame. Only *then* his bright blue eyes were open and his cheeks were rosy red from laughter. Matt touched Nate's exposed hand. It was still and cold. His palm looked puffy like it was made of rubber.

Mr. Calahan returned and squeezed Matt's shoulder. He moved around the bed and said a quiet hello to Hulk's grandmother. She returned the greeting and thanked him for coming, mumbling something about needing more faith in the room.

Matt's dad offered to pray and the group around the bed grabbed hands and bowed their heads. Matt peeked over at Hulk and saw his head bowed, too.

"Heavenly Father, we pray for Nathaniel today. We know you love him with all your heart. So today we pray that you would be with him and bring your healing power into his life. We know you are God and you are able to heal your creation. We stand in agreement, knowing that when two or more gather in prayer, you are here with us. Be with the Hooligans, too. We pray for your peace that passes understanding to flow through their lives. In Jesus' name, amen."

"Amen," the boys said.

"Amen," Grandma Hooligan said.

Hulk lifted his head, but didn't say anything.

A blond, female nurse entered the room, took some notes on the machine's readouts, and left again. Matt's dad continued to talk quietly to Grandma Hooligan as the QoolQuad watched Nate and studied the many machines hooked up to his bed.

Soon, Matt's dad looked at his watch and said they had to go so he could make an important appointment. As they said their good-byes and headed out the door, Matt stopped and looked back at Nate once more. He seized his dad's arm.

"Dad, can I stay?"

Mr. Calahan looked at his watch again. "You sure? Dinner's in an hour or so."

"Yeah. I'd like to stay if I can."

"If it's all right with the Hooligans, it's all right with me, Ace. When do you want me to pick you up?"

"Actually . . . can I just stay until he wakes up? Even if it's all night? I'd just . . . like to stay. We don't have school tomorrow."

"Well . . . I suppose. If you really want to. If it's all right with the Hooligans."

Matt stepped back into the room and crouched down beside Hulk. "Hey, you mind if I stay with you guys? I'd just like to be here, you know, praying for Nate . . . if you don't mind."

Hulk looked away then back at Matt. "What? What're ya gonna do? Fix everything with a wave of yer hand?"

Matt couldn't believe it. The guy was *such* a Neanderthal. "I know it's tough, I just—"

"Let me tell ya somethin'. Ya have no idea what it's like. Maybe if ya got outta your little comfort zone once in a while, you'd get it."

As Hulk's tone became more demeaning, Matt felt his blood begin to boil. He was about to let Hulk have it, to tell him what a bully he was, when he looked back at Nate. Suddenly, he remembered the Scripture Lamar had left for him: "But while he was still a long way off, his father saw him and was filled with compassion for him." Hulk was a long way off . . . and Matt knew he had to have compassion.

"Okay. Whatever," Matt gave in. "Look . . . let's forget all that for now, okay? Just tell me: Can I stay here and be with Nate? Because while you and I may not get along, I happen to care about your brother."

"Whatever, Calhan. I don't care. Just stay outta my face."

Matt smiled. "Great. You won't even know I'm here."

Matt told his dad the Hooligans approved his company. Mr. Calahan gave Matt twenty dollars in small bills and change for dinner and snacks. They all said they'd see Matt in the morning.

As they dismissed themselves, Lamar passed a note to Matt. "Check these out," he said. "I copied them from my Bible. Thought maybe you could share them with Nate."

Matt glanced at the list of Scriptures. "Thanks." Lamar was the one in their group, always thinking spiritually, always encouraging.

Matt made his way to the plush chair opposite Hulk, who was completely ignoring him now. He pulled off his backpack and sat down to read the note Lamar had given him.

> *Exodus 15:26 — "I am the Lord, who heals you."*
>
> *Psalm 118:17 — I will not die but live, and will proclaim what the Lord has done.*

Matt nodded. "Nate will not die but live," he whispered, "and he will proclaim what the Lord has done."

A half hour later, Mr. Hooligan returned to the room, reeking of cigarette smoke. He shot Matt a disapproving glance and then walked up and studied Nate.

Another half hour passed, Hulk's dad pacing the floor, his shoes providing a steady *tap, tap, tap, tap.* At last, he stopped in front of Hulk's chair. "You eat anything?" he asked.

"Not hungry," Hulk stated.

"Well, I am. If you don't eat now, don't gorge yourself later. You don't need any extra weight."

Matt found himself very thankful for the dad he had.

At 8:30 P.M., Matt noticed for the first time that his stomach was growling. He got up, tossed his backpack over his shoulder, and headed to the vending machines. Navigating the hospital corridors was a trick in itself and he retraced his steps more than once. At last, he found the machines, but the only food inside were Cheetos and Moon Pies. He wasn't sure exactly what a Moon Pie was, but he decided he'd force himself to eat a couple. At least then he could tell his mom he got his dairy for the day . . . or not.

The walk back to the room took him by a waiting room with several forlorn faces. Were they waiting to hear news about their own Nate? At the next hall, he took another wrong turn which took him by the chapel. He was surprised to see Mr. Hooligan sitting in the back row.

He stayed and watched him for a long moment, the man's frame frozen.

"God, we need your help," Matt whispered.

He continued down the hallway, more slowly this time, turning and peeking into the rooms as he passed them. He rarely saw anyone, but when he did, he also saw lots of tubes, or machines bleeping and blurping. A nurse passed him, pushing a young girl in a wheelchair who had bruises on her forehead and drool dripping down her chin. Matt turned another corner and stopped when he saw bed after bed of patients. He stepped back, over- whelmed at the sight. Certainly, none of them had chosen to be there, flat on their back, dis- abled. He found himself oddly thankful that he *wasn't* there, lying on his back . . . realizing it could just as well be him.

Matt wanted to help them, to heal all their injuries, to make everything right. But even with a special laptop, he didn't have that kind of power him- self. Not that he hadn't tried. Still, tonight he knew he had to help Nate in every way he could. He would pray for him. He would stand for him. He would believe for him.

Back in the room, Matt opened the paper Lamar gave him and read it again.

> *Exodus 15:26 — "I am the Lord, who heals you."*
>
> *Psalm 118:17 — I will not die but live, and will proclaim what the Lord has done.*

He carefully refolded the paper. Quietly, he pulled his laptop out of his backpack. As it booted, he watched Grandma Hooligan sit soundlessly, her lips moving as she prayed. Nate lay completely still. Hulk hadn't moved a muscle.

Matt could hear the wind stirring up outside. It was beginning to rain again. The drops hit the window, coming down stronger this time than they had just a day before. If this kept up, Matt imagined the local TV stations would be issuing flash flood warnings and other traumas that make the nightly news more interesting.

Once it was booted up, Matt opened the word processor and typed a simple line over and over. Each time he did, his finger flew over to the key with the clock on it. Part of him was tempted to feel helpless and alone, but he had a peace in his heart. He knew he had to do what he could, every moment he could. Into the night, again and again, as his fingers numbed and his eyes drifted, he typed:

```
Nate will not die but live.
Nate will not die but live.
Nate will not die but live.
Nate will not die but live.
Nate will not die but live.
Nate will not die but live.
Nate will not die but live.
```

No Business Like Dream Business

6

The wind blew crisply, slapping rain in every direction. It was coming down so hard, it felt as though small bits of glass were nicking Matt in the face. He stood strong, squinting into the wind, but refusing to let it push him backward. "When will it stop?" he shouted to Lamar, who stood beside him.

"I don't know!"

"But I want it to stop!"

Gill, camcorder in hand, stood on the other side of Matt. The wet rain soaked him and slid down his face. "Smile!" he yelled. "Everyone's watching you!"

Alfonzo appeared behind Gill, twirling a basketball on the end of his index finger. "¡Hola! ¡ Como esta!" he hollered.

Matt twisted his head back and saw Nate, lying on his bed, the sheets soaked through. Hulk sat beside the bed with his arms crossed.

"We have to stop the rain!" Matt shouted to his friends.

"I'll help," offered a voice behind Matt. He turned to see his dad, smiling, placing a caring hand on his shoulder.

"We have to stop it!" Matt cried.

Mr. Calahan nodded. "All right. Ready?"

"Yes!"

"One for the money . . . two for the show . . . three to get ready and . . ."

Barrrrringggg! Barrrrringggg!

"Oh, wait—I have to get the phone. Hello?"

Matt looked back at Nate again. His eyes grew wide as he saw his own face on Nate's body, which had turned a shade of deep blue.

"We have to stop it! We have to stop the storm!" Matt cried.

"We're trying!" Lamar spat.

"But it's not enough! We're not doing enough!"

"We're doing what we can!"

Suddenly a voice boomed that shook Matt from head to toe. "NATE WILL NOT DIE BUT LIVE!"

Matt's head fell back and his body jerked forward at once. He gasped for air and shook his head, trying to get his bearings. Then he spied Nate Hooligan in the hospital bed across the room, a tube lying across his face, breathing steadily. Matt shook his head and blinked, clearing his vision. He squinted and saw that Nate's eyes were open and he was looking at his grandmother, who was still faithfully by his side, holding his hand. On the other side of the bed, Hulk stood, mumbling something to his brother. To Matt's surprise, Hulk's dad was there, too, standing at the foot of the bed.

Matt swallowed hard. He could hear the rain beating against the window.

"You all right?"

Matt jumped and gasped, swallowing his shout.

"Dude! Sorry! Didn't want to give you the creepers."

Matt let his heart calm; it was just his youth pastor, Mick Ruhlen, who had just entered the room. His Chia Pet hair was bright green today, yet another expression of his individuality.

"Pastor Ruhlen! What are you doing here?"

"Came to see Nate, man. Part o' my pastoral duties."

"What time is it?"

"Eight-thirty A.M. Visitin' hours've started, dude. You been here all night?"

"I guess so."

"That's some yarn you're spinnin'," he noted, nodding.

Matt suddenly realized he'd left the laptop open, its screen declaring, "Nate will not die b . . ." Matt finished the sentence:

```
Nate will not die but live.
```

He hit the clock key. The golden icon of the clock quickly ticked forward, and then he shut the laptop.

"You know," Pastor Ruhlen said, "you can't just will something like that to happen, Matt. It's not mind over matter. It's a person."

Matt looked at his surfer/youth pastor for a long moment. He had hit the nail on the head more than he knew. It wasn't that the laptop wasn't working. It was that there were some things Matt couldn't change with a keystroke or two. Some things needed more than just a nudge of physical motion or a carefully planted suggestion. Some things needed—

"The power of prayer, man."

"Huh?"

Pastor Ruhlen popped his head to the side as if he were busting a groove. "Dude—you see Nate's up?"

Matt quickly turned his head and a smile formed on his face. "Wow."

"Power of prayer."

"Yeah."

Matt shoved his laptop into his backpack and drew the zipper from one side to another. He stood up and stretched, suppressing a yawn.

Together, Matt and Pastor Ruhlen walked over to the foot of Nate's bed. Mr. Hooligan scooted over by Grandma Hooligan. The boy's head pivoted and he stared at Matt. His blond hair was ruffled this way and that.

"Hi, remember me? I met you last week. I'm Matthew Roberts Calahan, but they call me Matt."

Nate's blue eyes lit up and a sweet smile crept across his face.

"He's sick, not dumb," Hulk threw in for good measure. "Of course he remembers ya."

When Hulk looked away, Matt shifted his eyes to Nate and mouthed the words, "Bo-bo head."

The boy smiled wide.

"How are you feeling, Nate?" Matt asked.

"I'm cold, but I feel all right. I'm in the hospital."

"I know it. We're all here because we want you to feel better."

"I have a TV up there with cable and I get ice cream sometimes. Maybe you can watch a basketball game with me later."

Matt about laughed. "I'd like that. You stay strong for me, okay?"

"I will."

Hulk shot Matt a glare, like he was already tired of his presence in the room. Matt winked at Nate and decided to give Hulk, his dad, and his grandmother some time to talk privately to him. "I'm gonna go get a . . . Moon Pie. Anyone want anything?"

"I could nibble on some grub. I'll join you," Pastor Ruhlen said, inviting himself.

"I didn't even know this cafeteria was here," Matt told Pastor Ruhlen. "This place is so huge."

Breakfast at the Enisburg Central Hospital cafeteria was just one step up from lunch at the Enisburg Junior High cafeteria. The difference was, the meat at the hospital was tender enough to cut. Taste, on the other hand, was about the same—like cardboard with bacon flavoring.

Matt discovered something else during his morning meal; his notorious youth pastor was a chatterbox at 8:30 A.M., while Matt was not.

"So you been here all night, huh, dude? You look like it."

"Mmm. I should have brought a comb."

Pastor Ruhlen leaned his lanky form toward Matt. "You bring any deodorant?"

Matt stopped chewing and pressed his arms closer to his body. His eyes widened. "Do I need some?"

"Ha! No—not implyin' anything, dude! I just know these are those 'formative' years, you know. Growing taller, pressin' into God, pressin' into life, starting to use stuff like deodorant. Shoot, man, you'll be shaving in no time."

A lady at the table across the way scrutinized Matt.

Matt leaned in. "I've been wearing deodorant for two years," he whispered.

"Ah, early bloomer. But you don't wanna talk about this, do ya? Let's talk about Nate. How you know that little guy?"

Matt was thrilled to change the subject. "Um, actually I don't really. I just met him last week. It's pretty hard to get to know him, really, with Hulk hovering over him."

"The Hulkster givin' you a hard time?"

"He's just being a . . . bo-bo head."

"Strong words."

"I don't know *what* his deal is. Listen to him when we go back to the room. His tone is like, 'You're nothin', Calhan.'" Matt paused a moment and calmed down. "But I'm not here for him. I'm here for Nate. I just wish there was something I could do. Everyone seems so depressed . . . and I guess they should be. I just . . ." Now Matt was turning into the chatterbox.

"Dude!" Pastor Ruhlen exclaimed. "You *are* doing something! You're here, man! You're the colossalest, most compassionate dude I know. I can see the love in every messed-up hair on your head."

Matt pulled his fingers through his hair. "Thanks. But I mean, I wish I could just *do* something." He took another bite of scrambled eggs.

"That's what I'm sayin'. You *are* doin' somethin'. Let me tell you something about compassion. Sometimes it develops strongest in silence. Just you being here—even not saying much—dude, it matters. Think about all the other chumps in this town. Where are they? At home watchin' Looney Tunes. But you—you're here. You're fulfilling the 2:52 vision. Like Jesus, you're growing in wisdom and stature, and in favor with God and man. You're doin' the smart thing. I'm proud of you."

"Thanks."

"No prob. Stirrin' you up, that's my job. Your job is just to be stirred."

Matt narrowed his eyes and smiled. "I have no idea what you're talking about."

Pastor Ruhlen winked. "It'll hitcha later."

On their way back to the room, Pastor Ruhlen and Matt slowed down when they spotted Nate's doctor, a tall man who looked Indian, talking to Mr. Hooligan. The doctor had dark, distinct eyebrows and a sharp chin. "I'm not going to lie to you, Mr. Hooligan," the doctor was saying. "Nate's awake now and in good spirits, but he's far from being well enough to go home."

"This is my boy," Harm Hooligan whispered emphatically. "Him and Hulk is all I got. You gotta do somethin', Doc."

The doctor noticed Pastor Ruhlen and Matt stop and put up his hands.

Mr. Hooligan looked over at them. He shook his head. "Ah, I don't care if they hear."

The doctor pursed his lips and made a clicking noise with his heel. "I'm going to have my staff run their tests again, but it doesn't look good. He's lost a lot of fluid and his heart is very weak. For a while, if it wasn't for our machines, I'm just not sure . . ."

Matt suddenly felt hollow inside.

"Don't lose hope," the doctor said. "I've seen miracles happen. But I don't want to put him on any more medication . . . and without a heart soon . . ." He shook his head.

Pastor Ruhlen put his hand on Matt's shoulder and they resumed the walk to Nate's room. Matt just wondered what else—if anything—he could possibly do. It seemed they had won a battle, but they were slowly losing the war.

Matt caught a ride home with Pastor Ruhlen after talking to Nate for a while. Unlike everyone else, Nate seemed completely relaxed about his condition, as if this were just a part of life. He was actually more concerned about catching the basketball game on TV than about how he was doing.

On the way home, Pastor Ruhlen asked Matt about the father/son retreat and Matt blew him off as politely as he could. Still, after seeing Hulk and his father interact, Matt was warming to the idea.

The rain was coming down in sheets, and Matt had to run from Pastor Ruhlen's car into his house. When he got inside, he realized that he hadn't even thanked him for the ride. *Well*, he thought, *now we're even for the deodorant comment.*

Matt showered, changed, and checked the battery life on his laptop. He was brushing his teeth when the doorbell rang. Mouth still full of toothpaste, he ran down the stairs and looked through the peephole. It was Isabel. Shoving his wet toothbrush into his jeans pocket, Matt opened the door. She smiled wide,

 her snow-white teeth twinkling. She held a black and white polka-dot umbrella over her head while the rain fell in a steady shower around her.

"Hwwwoo," Matt said, pressing his lips together, hoping and praying foamy toothpaste wasn't squishing out.

"Uh ... hi ..."

Matt smiled.

"Sugar?"

Matt nearly swallowed his mouthful of tooth-paste. *Did she just call me Sugar?* "How can I help you, Honey Muffin?" was on the tip of his tongue, but he realized he would spit toothpaste all over her if he spoke.

Isabel held out a measuring cup.

"Mmmm!" Matt exclaimed, realizing she *wanted* sugar. She wasn't making a statement about their relationship at all. Good thing his mouth had been full.

Matt grabbed the cup, put up his finger, and ran into the kitchen. He spit the toothpaste into the sink and finally was able to breathe. He filled the cup with sugar and ran back to the door where he smiled and held the cup out to her.

"Sorry," he said clearly. It was the first intelligible word he had ever said to Isabel. "I had toothpaste in my mouth." Then he realized she was standing outside and he had *made* her stand outside *in the rain* while he fetched the sugar. "Oh! You want to come in?"

Isabel shook her head and giggled.

"What?"

She bit her lip.

"I have toothpaste running down my chin, don't I?"

Isabel nodded. Matt wiped his mouth with the back of his hand and then winced. His mom always told him not to do that. He was striking three for three.

Both of them stood there silently for a moment. Then Isabel said, "Um . . . I wanted to tell you something, too. I just want you to know I really respect how you've been helping that little boy with the heart problem. Alfonzo told me how you stayed at the hospital all night and everything."

"Oh. It's really . . . nothing."

Isabel shook her head. "That's not true. In Mexico, when someone in your family is hurting, everyone comes to help them. But when we moved here, everything seemed different. People here don't see their relatives that often, don't eat with them, don't have time for them. But what you did was very nice. You reached out to someone and cared for him like family. It was very nice of you."

Matt felt the color rising to his cheeks.

"That's all. Just wanted to tell you that." She waved with her pinky and turned around. Then she stopped in her tracks and turned back to Matt. "Oh, and . . . thank you for being a good friend to my brother. Ever since Mama left, everything is just sports. He doesn't talk much."

"I noticed that."

She paused and then added, "He's starting to talk more."

Matt's heart was pounding. "How about you?" he asked.

Isabel took a deep breath and smiled. "I'm going to go make my cookies."

Matt returned the smile. "You'll have to save me one."

"Maybe." She twirled on her heel and returned home.

Well, he thought, *that was a nice ray of sunshine in an otherwise cloudy day.*

Twenty minutes later, after he'd recovered from the humiliation of foaming at the mouth like a rabid dog, Matt talked to Lamar on the phone. He shared the good news that Nate was awake again . . . and then the bad news that he still wasn't doing so well. Lamar said he, Gill, and Alfonzo wanted to visit Nate again, so Matt suggested they go back to the hospital after lunch.

"Just hop right into Ms. Whitmore's taxi cab, baby," Lamar's mother said when she picked him up later. Lamar was in the front with his mom, and Gill was in the backseat. Alfonzo ran over from his house across the street and crowded into the back with Matt and Gill. "Nuh-uh. This cab ain't goin' nowhere without your seat belts fastened. Get 'em on, boys, c'mon." There was no one safer than Lamar's mom. As she drove, she made constant comments about the slick roads, wondering what she was doing out in the 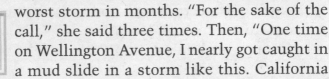 worst storm in months. "For the sake of the call," she said three times. Then, "One time on Wellington Avenue, I nearly got caught in a mud slide in a storm like this. California mud slide. I saw it happening right over my shoulder. Mud sliding down, carrying rocks and trees right onto the road. My-oh-my. In a storm just like this."

But Matt knew Ms. Whitman's inclination toward safety went deeper than a mud slide. Lamar's dad had been killed in an auto accident just two months before he was born. That was fourteen years ago, and her sadness had healed since then ... but still ... all it took was a bad storm to bring back the most difficult of memories. The entire way to the hospital, she never went over thirty miles per hour, so it took nearly twenty-five minutes to get there, which was a *lot* in a town the size of Enisburg.

Back in the hospital room, the TV above the bed was tuned into a basketball game. Alfonzo was thrilled since he had been watching it at his house.

The Slammer was playing and Alfonzo didn't want to miss a move. Nate's grandmother graciously sat and watched, too, but Hulk's dad was nowhere to be found. When the QoolQuad entered, Hulk groaned and slouched back down in the corner chair he'd lived in since he first arrived. Matt realized that Hulk was just outwardly expressing the way he felt on the inside: gloomy.

Gill told Nate a joke. Then he told him he was preparing to audition for a commercial downtown and to watch for him because he'd be famous one day. Alfonzo showed Nate a trick with his basketball—something he once saw the Harlem Globetrotters do. It made Nate laugh more than Gill's joke did.

Then, as Lamar shared a Scripture with Nate, Gill pulled Matt aside.

"You have your laptop in your backpack?"

"I *always* have my laptop in my backpack. Why?"

"I was thinking," Gill said.

"That can't be good."

"Ha-ha. Look. Maybe there's something special we can do for Nate."

"What do you mean?"

"I mean we're in the business of making dreams come true, right?"

"Right."

"So let's find out what his dream is. Maybe we can make it come true. At least we'd be doing *something*. Like Lamar always says, 'When God gives you a gift, you gotta use it.'"

Matt nodded and looked at Gill, his red hair standing up on end in the back. "That's actually a good idea," he said.

"I know it. I'm gonna have to get an agent."

Matt rolled his eyes. He moved over beside Lamar and waited for him to finish. Then he asked, "Hey, Nate, I have a question for you."

"K."

"If you could have one dream come true, what would it be?"

Nate thought for a long moment. "I want to go to Mars," he said finally.

Matt blinked and looked at Gill. Gill looked at Lamar. Lamar looked at Alfonzo. Alfonzo looked at Matt.

"Let's talk about something a little more realistic," Matt coaxed. "If there was one dream that you could really have right now, what would it be?"

Nate thought for a minute as his eyes moved around the room. They settled on the TV screen— the Slammer giving a sound bite at halftime: "Yes, as we pull togethew as a team, I believe we can wock this game."

Nate giggled. "I want to meet the Slammer. That would be *soooo* cool."

Matt blinked. He looked at Lamar. Lamar looked at Gill. Gill looked at Alfonzo. Alfonzo looked at Matt. "Actually," he said, "this is a local game. The Slammer's in town."

Matt looked at the television set.

"All right, Nate," he promised, "We'll get the Slammer to come meet you."

"Whoa!" Hulk shouted, jumping up. "Are ya crazy? No one just 'gets' the Slammer. Don't be making promises like dat, Calhan. Dat's impossible!"

"As impossible as you passing an English test?" Matt shot back. "I'll get the Slammer."

Nate clapped. "Slam-mer! Slam-mer!"

Matt was ready to use the laptop in a way that he *knew* it would work.

Gill winked at Nate. "You'll like the Slammer. He's a redhead. And he's famous."

Lamar leaned into Matt. "You sure you know what you're promising?"

"I have no idea," Matt replied. "But I think I'm about to find out."

Alfonzo's Challenge

7

Lamar's mom was a real sport about chauffeuring them to the Enisburg Convention Center. When Lamar told her their purpose—to see if they could get the Slammer to visit Nate—she thought it sounded like a difficult venture. But their enthusiasm overwhelmed her—and she had seen God do some pretty amazing things for her son. So off they went to try and make a dream come true. The rain was getting heavier and Ms. Whitmore was driving slower, making Matt and his friends restless. When they finally arrived at the convention center, she asked the boys how long they'd be.

"Maybe an hour," Lamar said.

"All right," she returned. "I'm going to head next door to Target and do some shopping. I'll be back in one hour—right here. My prayers are with you."

"Thanks, Ma," Lamar said.

82

The boys bolted out of the car and into the convention center, getting half-soaked in the process. They didn't have tickets, so they couldn't get into the main arena, but that didn't matter.

"There are plenty of other spots around here to meet the Slammer," Matt pointed out. "Let's find somewhere secluded. I don't want a thousand fans trying to get his autograph while we talk to him."

"Right!" Gill agreed. Then he asked, "What do you mean *secluded*?"

"Have you been paying attention in English class?" Matt asked.

"Yes," Gill said, sounding put out.

Matt wasn't about to get into another vocabulary lesson. "I want somewhere that's away from everything else. Somewhere quiet. Somewhere private."

Alfonzo still held his faded orange basketball. "How about somewhere with a hoop?"

Matt nodded. "I like that. It'll work well into the story I write to get the Slammer into the room."

"Let's do it," Lamar agreed, clapping his hand into his fist.

Gill surveyed the area and paused when he saw a security guard. "I'll find us just the place," he pledged, and walked over to the guard.

"What's he gonna do?" Matt whispered to Lamar.

"I have *no* idea."

A minute and a half later, the security guard gave Gill a high five, smiling brightly. Gill returned to the group and reported, "There's a small practice gym this way."

Matt grinned. "How'd you—? What'd you—?"

"It's the Gillespie charm," Gill said, rubbing his fingernails on his shirt. Then, "I just told him I had connections to the Great Gillespie, the security guard who foiled the Baker Brothers. He was quite impressed. Wants me to have my dad send him an autographed picture."

"You're kidding."

Gill waved to the security guard who waved back, a goofy grin on his face.

"You're not kidding," Matt stated. "Okay. Great work, Gill. I guess fame runs in the family. Take us to the practice gym."

"This-a-way!" Gill waved them on.

The practice gymnasium was the same size as the Enisburg Junior High gym, but with four basketball hoops that folded down from the ceiling instead of two. All four were fully extended, probably because there was a big game going on in the main arena. Though the walls were made of cement, they could still hear the crowd of thousands cheering for the teams. Matt wished he could watch the game, but he had more important things to do.

While Alfonzo and Gill played a little one-on-one (largely in Alfonzo's favor), Matt wrote the scenario with Lamar by his side.

> At the end of the basketball game, the Slammer felt he needed a breath of fresh air. He'd played hard. He'd played good. He needed some time alone. So, to get away from the crowd, he strolled nonchalantly into the practice gym to shoot a few hoops. When he got there, he met four charming guys.

"Who's that?" Lamar asked

"Us!"

"Oh, right."

Matt hit the clock key and the golden clock flashed on screen, ticking forward furiously. It was set. Now they just had to wait for the game to end.

Thirty-five minutes later the boys were still waiting in the practice gym.

"I thought the game was about over," Matt said to no one in particular.

"Must've gone into overtime," Alfonzo guessed. He shot for the basket, but the ball hit the rim and bounced off. Gill caught the rebound and double-dribbled enough times to make Alfonzo's eyes cross. He shot for the basket and missed it by a mile.

Matt looked at his watch. "Well, it'd better end soon, or we'll miss our ride."

Less than five minutes later, a door on the other side of the small gym popped open. Matt, Lamar, Gill, and Alfonzo jumped, then froze when they saw the giant redheaded man in a bright purple tank top and shorts. He was so tall, he had to duck to get through the doorway. The towel around his neck looked like a washcloth compared to his body. Matt gulped. Alfonzo dropped his basketball.

"Sowwy, boys, didn't mean to intewwupt," he said in his signature Fudd-esqe voice. He turned to leave.

"N–no! Wait a second!" Matt cried.

The giant man they called "The Slammer" turned around. He looked Matt over, his sweaty brow dripping onto the floor.

"Yeah?"

"Um, we wanted to talk to you."

"Ah, you want an autogwaph?"

"Um, no, we—"

"Absolutely!" exclaimed Gill, who unzipped a pocket on Matt's backpack and took out one of his school notebooks.

The Slammer grinned from ear to ear as he took the notebook and pen. He asked Gill to whom he should sign it. Gill said, "Sign it, 'To my greatest fan.'"

Matt looked at Gill. As the Slammer signed the notebook, Matt whispered to his friend, "You said yesterday that you didn't even know who he was."

"I don't!" Gill whispered back. "But he's famous and has red hair. Besides . . . just think how much I can get for this on eBay."

The Slammer started to return the pad, but Matt pushed it back at him. "Me too!"

"Yeah, me too!" Lamar joined in.

"And one for my sister!" Alfonzo pushed.

A minute later when the Slammer finished signing, he thanked the four boys. "Well, I'd bettew be going. I played hawd tonight and I played good. I think I need some time alone."

"Wait!" Matt shouted. "Um, we wanted to talk to you. To ask you a favor."

"I don't have time fow tips wight now. It's waining pwetty bad. I gotta go befowe it's too wough out fow my choppew."

"Your *what?*" Gill asked, his eyes wide.

"My choppew."

"You have a choppew, eh, helicopter?"

"Yeah. Well, nice to meet you, boys."

Matt couldn't believe his boldness, but he grabbed the Slammer's sweaty arm. "No! Just listen. We have a bigger favor to ask—bigger than basketball tips. We know a little boy—"

"His name's Nate," Lamar interjected.

"And he's got a serious heart problem. He's waiting for a new heart, but they don't know when it will come. He may not have much time left and . . . his biggest dream in life is to meet you, Mr. Slammer. Will you come with us to the hospital to see him?"

The Slammer's head dropped. He stared at the floor and he ran his giant hand over his red head. "Boys, I appweciate what you'we twying to do, but . . . I just finished a hawd game. It's waining bad outside. I just can't. Sowwy." He pulled away from Matt's grip and started to walk away.

"But—"

"I'm sowwy."

Alfonzo spoke up. "Doesn't matter. He's not that good of a basketball player anyway," he said. "I could beat him any day."

All heads turned to Alfonzo. Matt's mouth dropped in disbelief. The Slammer turned around, his red eyebrows in the air.

"What?"

"Oh, yeah," Alfonzo boasted. "He's all tired after that game. I could beat him."

"Nobody beats the Slammew," the Slammer said.

"Um, he doesn't mean what he's saying," Lamar defended his friend.

"Sure I do!" Alfonzo assured, smiling wide. He stepped forward. "Tell you what," he charged the Slammer, "let's you and I go one-on-one."

The Slammer chuckled. "You—against me?"

"Yeah. And if I win, you come to visit our friend Nate. If you win, we won't bug you anymore."

"You—against me?" the Slammer repeated.

Matt couldn't believe what he was hearing. "Um, Alfonzo," he whispered, "he may talk like Elmer Fudd, but he doesn't play like Elmer Fudd, remember? I mean, his hand is bigger than your head, so maybe . . ."

Alfonzo's eyes shifted to the laptop.

Matt's eyes followed. He smiled and spoke louder. "Maybe this is an opportunity he wouldn't want to miss."

The Slammer smiled wide and threw his towel on the bench. "That's exactly wight."

Matt slid onto the bench. "Great. While you two play . . . I'll just be over here writing. Excuse me."

Bounce! Bounce! Bounce! Swish!

Bounce! Bounce! Steal! Bounce! Bounce! Swish!

Out on the practice gym basketball court, the Slammer was running heads and tails around Alfonzo. He'd steal the ball, jump higher than Alfonzo could ever hope to jump, and then swish the ball right into the basket. To show off once, he even stole the ball with his long arms and then jumped up and slam-dunked it, living up to his name.

"Hurry up!" Gill coaxed Matt. "Slammer's already got him ten to zip!"

"Don't rush me!" Matt hushed back. "Allow the writer room to create!"

"Well, you'd better create fast, or we'll be sweeping Alfonzo off the floor!"

Matt typed:

> The Slammer was good. He had the game . . . but then it happened. Alfonzo got into the Zone. Nothing was going to distract him now. Though he was behind, he was confident. Because just as he was getting into the Zone, the Slammer was getting out of it.

Bounce! Bounce! The Slammer reached out to steal the ball, but Alfonzo, seemingly getting his second wind, whipped the ball between his legs and caught it behind him, throwing the Slammer off. He doubled back, then forward, and shot. The Slammer leaped sideways, but missed and . . .

> It was good! Nothin' but net!

It was good, all right. The ball shot through the hoop, hitting nothing but the bottom of the net.

"Two to twelve!" Gill shouted, as if the victory was already won.

Matt wiped his forehead. He suddenly found himself thankful for all those finger races in his sixth grade typing class.

"What's game?" The Slammer looked slightly bewildered.

"Twenty-one?" Alfonzo suggested.

Slammer smiled. "Let's do it. I'm alweady halfway thewe."

Bounce! Bounce! Bounce! Bounce! The Slammer shifted left then right. He shot past Alfonzo and went in for the kill.

Bap! The ball popped off the side of the hoop, and flew right back into Alfonzo's hands. He backtracked, then came forward and took a three—and made it!

The Slammer jumped up and—*bap!*—the basketball hit the rim and flew back onto the court.

Alfonzo caught the rebound, stepped back, and then shot the ball forward for a three-pointer.

"Five to twelve!" Gill shouted.

The Slammer shook his head and looked at Alfonzo, disbelieving.

"I'm nearly halfway there," Alfonzo said, passing the ball to the Slammer.

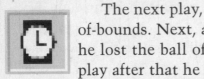 The next play, the Slammer stepped out-of-bounds. Next, as he was driving the lane, he lost the ball off the side of his foot. The play after that he actually passed the ball to Alfonzo by accident. That one was Gill's idea.

Suddenly the score was 11–12 and the Slammer called a time-out.

"I'm wiped," he said. Then to Alfonzo, "And, hey, you awen't bad."

"I put my whole self into the game."

"Suwe do."

The Slammer chugged down a long drink of water from a nearby fountain. When he came back, to the QoolQuad's surprise, the Slammer gave in.

"Hey, bwo, let's call it a game."

"But I didn't beat you yet."

"And you'we not going to eithew," the Slammer said with a smile. "I'm quitting while I'm ahead. I don't want it getting out that I might have gotten beat by a sixteen-yeaw-old."

"I'm only fourteen."

"Gweat . . ."

"But what about the deal?"

The Slammer picked up his towel and wiped his head and arms. "I'm gonna gwant you youw wequest—not because you won . . . but because I feel fow youw sick fwiend."

"Thank you," Matt said.

"You'we welcome."

Matt looked at his watch. If Lamar's mom was on time—and she always was—she had already been sitting outside for eight minutes.

"Now we just have to figure out how to get us all in your mom's car," Matt said to Lamar.

The Slammer laughed. "Kid, I don't fit in no one's caw. I'll meet you thewe in my choppew. Any of you wanna wide with me?"

Matt shook his head, thinking of the helicopter stunt team he'd seen on TV. "Yeah, right. In this storm? I'll stick to the ground."

"We got him!" Lamar announced to his mother as the boys piled into the car.

The smile on her face burst wide open. "You did! All right, boy! Where is he?"

"He's taking his personal helicopter over!" Gill told her. "Is that cool or what? Carrot-top with a copter! We rule!"

Lamar interrupted. "Ma—he said we could fly with him if we want. Can we?"

"Lamar Larry Whitmore, have you lost your senses? Look at this weather. We shouldn't be driving in it, let alone flying."

"That's what I'm saying," Matt threw in for good measure. No aerial acrobatics for him.

"So I take it that's a no?" Lamar confirmed.

"A *big* N-O. We can meet him there."

"All right, Ma."

Ms. Whitmore pulled out slowly, then hit the brakes when a car zipped by, spitting water. It broke into a slide and the driver caught the wheel just in time. Ms. Whitmore took a deep breath. "Now you boys stay quiet. I need to be able to hear Jesus when I'm driving today."

"Maybe it'd be safer flying," Lamar suggested.

His mother shot him a look that made Matt turn away. He'd seen that look on his own mother before. You don't mess with *that* look.

"Here we go," Ms. Whitmore said. Then she smiled wide again. "I've never met a real celebrity. This'll be exciting!"

Hello, evewybody!"

As the Slammer entered, ducking his head, the jaws of everyone in Nate's room hit the floor. Nate's eyes were as big as softballs. Hulk's knees started shaking like Jell-O. Hulk's grandmother yelped. It was priceless. It was a Kodak moment.

"You must be Nate," the huge basketball player said, making his way across the room in two steps.

"You . . . you came!" Nate squealed.

"I wouldn't have missed meeting you," the Slammer said.

Hulk grabbed the Slammer's hand and shook it vigorously. "Hulk Hooligan," he introduced himself. "I'm your biggest fan!"

"And I'm youws." The Slammer grabbed a chair, scooted it up beside the bed, and started talking to Nate and Hulk.

"Mission accomplished," Gill boasted to his friends. "We really should go into business. Qool-Quad, Inc. 'We make dreams come true.' We should put that on our Web page that it's taking *forever* for Matt to write."

Lamar slugged Gill playfully in the arm. Lamar's mom, waiting to drive them home, giggled. Matt just smiled. Yes, typing a key here, typing a key there, and they made a small dream come true. *Well,* Matt thought, *it was a big dream for Nate.* Still, seeing the boy lying in the hospital bed, his face tinted blue, broke Matt's heart. He felt like their best-played effort was nothing but a Band-Aid that just couldn't stop the bleeding. Matt imagined that Hulk and his family would still have to face the inevitable.

Gill seemed to sense Matt's mood and pulled him aside. "Hey, why not just type that a heart is found?"

"You know I can't do that," Matt whispered back. "For a heart to be found, someone else has to lose theirs. And I can't make that happen. Remember our Honor Code rule number 4: I have to make sure my words—spoken *and* written—are always well thought out. And I've thought about it. And that's not right. Now if we *had* a heart, I'd type everything I could to make sure the procedure went well."

Gill nodded. "I guess you're right."

"I know he's right," Lamar threw in, joining the hushed conversation. "He's being responsible."

"Doesn't make it easy," Matt admitted.

"I know."

The Indian doctor entered the room, scanning his clipboard. When he looked up and saw the Slammer, he gasped. "You! You! You're the . . . Slammer!"

"Yeah, nice to meet you." The Slammer extended his hand. They shook and started talking.

Finally the doctor drew away. "I have to tell Nurse Tunis you're here. She's a big fan." Then on the side, he said to the QoolQuad, "He says you boys brought him here. That was a very nice thing you did. It's nice to see smiles on my patients' faces."

Matt looked at Nate again. He was smiling big, but his cheeks seemed puffier than even earlier that morning. His breathing was noticeably labored, especially with the excitement.

The doctor exited the room and Matt let out a long breath. "I need to get out of here and get a Moon Pie. Anyone coming?"

"I'm game," Gill and Alfonzo said at the same time.

The four boys made their way down the hall to the snack machine. Matt knew exactly where it was by now—no more aimlessly wandering around the hospital. When they got there, everyone placed an order for Moon Pies. Matt had started a trend.

"Eww—ever have any of those Pooka Dookas?" Gill pointed to a package of Pooka Dookas—animal-shaped cookies with bright green jelly inside. Matt couldn't quite tell what the jelly was made of . . . just some kind of fake sugar goop.

"I stay away from those," Matt said.

"Tell me about it! I hate their ads. They go, 'Pooka Dookas are supa-dupa!' and I think, 'Nuh-uh. Pooka Dookas make-a you puke-a!'"

The boys laughed. Matt thanked Gill for sharing.

"Hey," Lamar said, biting into his Moon Pie, "where's Mr. Hooligan anyway? Is he ever in the room?"

"Not much," Matt said. "C'mon, I'll show you."

Matt rounded two corners and then stopped. He turned to the large colored windows and nodded. Inside, Harm Hooligan sat at the back of the chapel, his back to the boys.

"This is where he goes?" Lamar questioned.

"He either comes here or goes outside and smokes," Matt said.

Lamar stated, "You know, *there's* a guy who needs to go on that father/son retreat with his sons."

Matt groaned. "I don't know. You think it will be any good? My dad and I have never gotten into stuff like that very well. He's pretty busy."

"If I had a dad, I'd be there in a heartbeat," Lamar said.

"Don't look at me," Gill said, "I'm with Matt."

Alfonzo shrugged. "I'm going."

All four boys turned to Alfonzo and said, "You're going?"

"You don't even go to our church," Matt added.

"Your youth pastor asked me to go. He and your head pastor came by our house to invite us to your church. Dad said we're looking around, but the retreat sounds like fun. We like stuff like that."

If Alfonzo attended Matt's church, he'd probably go to his youth group. And if he went, his sister Isabel would probably start going too . . . which wouldn't be so bad . . . but then again Matt was already pretty uncomfortable there and . . .

"You think he's praying for a miracle?" Gill asked, bringing the subject back to Mr. Hooligan.

"We all are," Matt replied. "If there's a way, God will show it to us."

"Well, he'd better hurry," Gill pointed out. "He'd just better hurry."

"So sad," the female nurse was saying. "It's so close, but there's nothing we can do."

Matt and his friends were passing by when Matt overheard the two nurses talking.

"That *is* sad," the male nurse said. "A heart so close."

Matt halted in his tracks. Lamar ran into him. Gill ran into Lamar. Alfonzo ran into Gill.

"Did you hear that?" Matt asked his friends. They all shook their heads. Matt approached the nurses. "Excuse me," he interrupted. "Were you talking about Nate Hooligan?"

The nurses looked at each other as if trying to determine who let the cat of the bag. "Um ... well ..."

"It's all right," Matt said. "I'm just curious."

Suddenly a deep voice spoke up behind the boys. "It's true." Matt turned to see the Indian doctor. "We haven't said anything because we don't usually like getting anyone's hope up before it gets to the hospital. In this case, I'm glad we haven't said anything. And I need you boys to promise me you won't say anything either. It could be devastating."

Matt's face wrinkled. "What's going on?"

"We found a heart," the doctor explained.

"You *what?*" Gill shouted.

"Shhh!" everyone shushed.

"Sorry."

"It was flown in from Nevada to our airport," the doctor continued. "Normally, we CareFlight them here, but this storm caught us off guard. The airport has shut down and advised CareFlight to stay on the ground, too."

"So why not drive it here?" Lamar asked.

"Well, until about an hour ago, it was on its way. We loaded it aboard an ambulance, but—have you boys been outside?—it's a constant downpour out there. The roads have flash flooded and . . . it seems our ambulance is stuck near a large mud slide. They just can't get through. And until things clear up, no one has been able to get to them. We've tried everything, please understand."

"What if I can find a way?" Matt pushed. He could feel Lamar's eyes on him.

"Son, I'm serious, we've tried everything. We'll have to wait until morning."

"What if morning's too late?"

"It could be, but— "

"What would it take?"

"Right now? A miracle."

"Well, *Miracles 'R' Us!*" Gill spouted.

Lamar snatched the Moon Pie out of Gill's hand. "You do *not* need any more sugar."

Matt thought about his dad, helping his friend Harry out when he needed it most. His mom had said his dad had performed a miracle by turning his compassion into action. Matt smiled.

"Tell me . . . where is this ambulance stranded— exactly?"

The Dangerous Flight

9

No! You awe not taking my choppew out in this stowm! No!"

"But it's the *only* way we can get the heart! Nate's life may count on it!"

"He's fine! He can wait until mowning!"

Out in the hall, Matt, Lamar, Gill, and Alfonzo had the Slammer pinned. Matt grabbed the Slammer's arm for the second time that day. "We don't *know* that he can wait until morning."

"Have you looked outside?" the Slammer insisted. "It's waining cats and dogs! I could get killed out thewe!"

"You won't get killed out thewe," Gill assured.

"You can't guawantee that."

"Yes, we can," Matt said.

"What? No, you can't."

"Okay." Matt shifted his backpack on his shoulder. "But, look, you can do it. You're the Slammer!"

Lamar added, "You have to do it—for the children of the world!"

Alfonzo added, "You have to do it—for the athletes of the world!"

Gill added, "You have to do it—for the redheads of the world!"

"Fowget all that," the big man said, waving his hand. "You'we not getting me woped into this."

"Fine," Matt said.

"Fine."

"Perfect."

"Pewfect."

At once, Matt, his friends and the Slammer jumped at the sound of machines shrieking from Nate's room. The doctor and three nurses rushed past them, the doctor barking orders that Matt had only heard on TV medical dramas. Stuff like "Stat!" "Gimme four cc's!" and "Pulse!"

As they stood stunned in the hallway, the medical crew shot back out of the room, rolling Nate's bed between them. They zipped through the hall, right past the QoolQuad. Matt barely caught a second's glimpse of Nate's bright blue eyes staring at him.

Hulk, Lamar's mother, and Hulk's grandmother followed the medical crew out of the room and stopped in the hall. Nate was wheeled behind two doors that declared "STOP Enisburg Medical Staff ONLY." The hallway was suddenly silent. Matt could hear the beating of his own heart. "What . . . what happened?" he asked finally.

"He went into arrest," Hulk said with a raspy voice. "Dis may be it. If only dey had found a heart. Guess God had other plans."

Matt, Lamar, Gill, and Alfonzo all looked up at the Slammer, who was visibly shocked. His face contorted for a moment and he caught his breath. He pushed his palm into his right eye and wiped. Then his face hardened.

He put his mammoth hand on Matt's shoulder. "So, guys, tell me . . . where is this ambulance stranded—exactly?"

BAM! The door to the roof crashed open and the chill of the hard evening rain and wind rushed into the hallway, slapping the group in the face. The sky was dark and ominous.

"Go! Go!" Slammer ordered his pilot, who, a minute ago, had been enjoying a cappuccino in the hospital cafeteria.

The pilot, a thin black man who looked as if he could have been a basketball player himself, ran forward through the rain toward the helicopter. He slipped once, making everyone wince, but quickly got back up and jumped inside. The Slammer pulled the hospital door shut and turned to the group. "I'm going with my pilot to get this heawt because someone has to wun out to get it, and I need him to stay in the choppew. But don't wowwy. I've faced wowse stowms than this on the basketball couwt. Nothing stops the Slammew!" Then, right on cue, as the whir of the helicopter broke through the sound of the rain, he shouted, "I'll be back!"

The group of friends and family burst onto the roof, cheering him on. The wind and blowing rain from the helicopter's blades nearly blinded them all. But they endured the torment to show him their support.

Matt huddled in the back of the helicopter. Strapped in a seat, and shivering from the wet and the cold, he was well-hidden under a blanket.

"You can do it!" Gill shouted.

"Our prayers are with you!" Lamar chimed in.

"Go, Slammer! Go!" Alfonzo added.

"Then Hulk asked, "Hey, where's Calhan?"

Matt huddled in the back of the helicopter. Strapped in a seat, and shivering from the wet and the cold, he was well-hidden under a blanket. He could see out through a peephole, while concealing the glow of his laptop's screen. This was most certainly the stupidest and boldest thing he had ever done in his life. But he knew he was the only one who could do it. He was the one entrusted with the laptop.

Boom! Matt nearly jumped out of the seat when the helicopter lifted off the hospital helipad. His stomach sunk and he felt sick. He couldn't see much out his peephole, but he could see that they were rising—and he sure could *feel* it. The rotors roared as they spun and the rain sounded like bullets being fired from all sides. Like in his dream, they were standing against the storm that was trying to take Nate's life. *Pop! Pop! Pop! Pop! Pop! Pop! Pop!* Rain hit the helicopter. Matt was sure this was an exercise in futility . . . or would be without the help he held in his hands.

"The Skoggan Stweet bwidge," Matt heard the Slammer informing his pilot of their destination. That's where the ambulance was blocked in—a mud slide on one side, a flood on the other.

"I can barely see!" the pilot exclaimed. "Man, it's bad out there. You sure this is a good idea?"

Matt quickly typed:

```
On their rescue mission, they didn't
lose hope. The Slammer and his pilot
were about to save a boy's life. It was
a matter they didn't take lightly at
all. No, not at all.
```

Finally, the Slammer said, "This may not be a good idea, but it's the wight idea."

The pilot nodded. "All right. You're the boss."

Matt smiled. It was nice to have a bit of control.

Sha-POW!!

A brilliant flash of light blew through the atmos-
phere, followed by a deafening crack. Matt screamed,
but the men up front didn't hear him because they
were screaming, too. The helicopter lurched right
and cascaded down. The pilot pulled sharply on the
controls and slapped buttons all over the cockpit.

"C'mon! C'mon!" he cried, desperate. "Pull up!
Pull up!"

Matt's mind raced, but he forced himself to focus.
He glued his fingers to the keyboard and typed:

```
%y3-8o95 h33e3e d9j549ol
```

Matt's eyes popped as he stared at the screen. The
helicopter continued to dive. *What was going wrong?
What had happened to the laptop?*

He quickly looked down at the keyboard. His fingers were on the wrong row.

"Focus!" he commanded himself. Quickly, he
typed,

```
The pilot needed control. He said a quick
prayer and then jerked at the steering
column. Immediately, it re-engaged and
the helicopter leveled out, much to the
relief of its frenzied passengers.
```

He pressed the clock key. *Sha-POW!* Like the lightning, the laptop went into effect. The pilot jerked the steering column up and pressed some buttons. Just as Matt wrote, the helicopter leveled out. The pilot took it back up and angled to the left. Matt felt a huge rush of relief. "Don't evew do that again," the Slammer ordered his pilot in a breathless voice.

"You don't have to tell me," the pilot replied.

Matt leaned back for a second and listened to the rain hitting the helicopter. Suddenly he found huge solace in it, compared to the lightning and thunder he could hear in the near distance. *Okay*, Matt thought, *so I can't control things. I just "nudge" them a little.*

As they flew, the copter shuddered left and right, the sound of the rain deafening. Matt refused to take his hands off the laptop. If he was the daredevil performing aerial artistry in a helicopter, he wasn't taking any chances. Every time he started to think about how high they were or how dangerous the situation was, he just kept remembering Nate. He kept envisioning that smiling, rosy-cheeked face popping into the window frame of his house. He kept envisioning the faces of all those patients at the hospital. He had to do what he could.

"Thewe it is!" the Slammer shouted, pointing down. "See? He's flashing the emewgency lights at us!"

Reflections of reds and whites flashed in the rain. The helicopter dropped once again, but this time on purpose, as they made their way to the ground.

"Watch the powew lines!" the Slammer shouted.

The helicopter jerked left, then right, then left again as the pilot attempted to land between the power lines on either side of the street.

> The pilot, completely alert, used his panther-like reflexes to settle the helicopter right on the street in front of Skoggan Street bridge.

The helicopter set down softly, even in the midst of the storm. Matt let out a long, thankful breath. The Slammer let out a long, thankful breath. The pilot let out a long, thankful breath.

The pilot reached over to open the door on his side of the helicopter, but the Slammer stopped him. "I'll get it," he said. "You've put in enough wowk fow one day." Then he pulled his jacket up to his neck, opened the door, and ran to the ambulance. Matt opened his peephole wider to see what was going on. It looked like the Slammer was talking to the ambulance drivers. They were shouting to one another, as it was all they could do in the storm. One of the medical men jumped out of the ambulance and ran to the back of the vehicle.

Sha-POW! Matt jumped as another burst of lightning shot down from the sky, thundering through the street. He thanked God they were safe on the ground.

Snap! Pop!

What was that?

Pop! Pop! Pop!

"Oh, no," the pilot whispered.

Oh, no? What did he mean, *Oh no?*

The pilot threw open his door, getting pounded by the wind and rain.

"Slammer!" he hollered. "Slammer!"

"What?"

"The power lines! They're coming down!"

Matt's eyes shifted to the tall poles standing beside the street. One had sparks shooting out of a power box at the top. The huge log the box hung on was completely split in half. It was weighting on the other poles near it. They were leaning in. Toward the helicopter.

No, they were *falling in.*

10

Thump! Thump!

The pilot had the helicopter roaring. The air it stirred seemed to rock the power lines even more. They swayed back and forth like rocking chairs, closer and closer to the helicopter's blades.

The Slammer spun around and grabbed a small cooler from the back of the ambulance.

> The Slammer looked right, looked left, and then let his basketball instincts take over. Holding the cooler close to his chest, he skirted through the rain as fast as he could and slam-dunked himself into the helicopter just in time.

The Slammer held the cooler in his hands. He cradled it to his chest and then shouted something

Matt couldn't distinguish. He charged forward, toward the helicopter, each step splashing mud and water everywhere.

"Go! Go! Go!" the medical man at the back of the ambulance shouted, hitting the truck, trying to get the attention of the driver at the front.

The pilot held Slammer's door open and Slammer leaped into the side of the helicopter, pulling the door shut behind him.

"Hit it!" the Slammer shouted. "Get this choppew off the gwound!"

Crrrraaaaccck! Pop! The power lines gave way and came tumbling down, each one pulling down the next like dominoes. Matt started to type, but his fingers couldn't fly fast enough. The pilot threw the helicopter in gear and pulled up, angling sideways at the same time. On the ground, the ambulance spun and squealed in the mud, jolting only a few feet at a time.

The helicopter pulled up and out of the trap, just as the medical men jumped out of the ambulance and 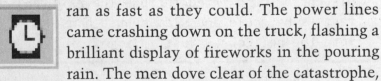 ran as fast as they could. The power lines came crashing down on the truck, flashing a brilliant display of fireworks in the pouring rain. The men dove clear of the catastrophe, and as the pilot jolted the helicopter to safety, Matt saw them give Slammer a thumbs-up.

Matt quickly took advantage of the free moment.

> During the trip back, the pilot and the
> Slammer were more alert than ever. They
> used their vast experience to bring the
> crew and the heart back to Enisburg
> Central Hospital safely.

They flew through the air at top speed, and Matt shivered as a chill crawled down his spine. The rain hit the helicopter like shards of glass, not helping to calm his nerves. They were so close ... Matt didn't want anything to stop them now.

The pilot weaved left and then right for what seemed like an eternity. Thunder cracked nearby. Matt started to feel sick to his stomach. Then, just as his whole body was starting to ache, he spotted lights up ahead. Lights on top of a tall building. The Enisburg Central Hospital.

The pilot squawked something into his radio and a moment later, Matt felt them hovering again, ready to set down.

Staying in the shadows, Matt followed the Slammer as he raced into the hospital, soaked to the core, triumphantly holding the cooler in his hands. He passed it to a medical assistant, who ran off with it. Lamar, Gill, Alfonzo, Lamar's mom, Hulk, and Hulk's grandmother cheered. This time Hulk's dad was there ... and even he was smiling. Everyone then returned to Nate's room to wait for news, except Lamar, Gill, and Alfonzo, who hung around out in the hall.

> **"Sometimes compassion means action,"** Matt said plainly.

"Hey, did I miss anything?" Matt asked, sneaking up behind them.

Alfonzo slapped Matt on the back. "Matt! All right!"

"Where have you been?" Lamar demanded.

"Just ... outside," Matt said with a smirk on his face. He was dripping wet.

"You are my hero," Gill said.

"Do you know how crazy that was?" Lamar, the voice of reason, interrupted. "Man, you're soaked!"

"Sometimes compassion means action," Matt said plainly.

"Well, let's take some action and get you dried off," Lamar said. As they made their way to the rest room, Lamar grabbed a stack of towels off a cart. "By the way," he added with a wink, "nice job."

Matt smiled. "When God gives you a gift, you've gotta use it."

"Word up."

"I'm gonna show you how to play some sewious basketball, soon as you get up and wunning awound."

"All right!" Hulk exclaimed.

"I'm not talking to you, man! I'm talking to youw bwother!"

"Yeah!" Nate hooted, shoving his thumb into his chest. "He's talking to me!"

A week had passed, the rain had mostly dried up, and the Slammer was back in town. He had contacted the QoolQuad to double-check on Nate's room at the hospital. When they arrived, Hulk's dad went outside to smoke, but Hulk welcomed them in to see his little brother, who was doing *very* well.

"How much longer will he be here?" Matt asked Hulk.

"Probably as long as he can stay here and act like he's still sick. Workin' the system to get as much green Jell-O as he wants."

"He learned from the best," Matt stated with a wink.

Hulk's eyebrows dodged in and out, as if he were unsure if Matt was making fun of him or not.

Nate giggled, his blue eyes flashing. Hulk returned to his chair.

The Slammer's pilot popped into the room. "Hey, boss—reporters in the lobby."

"Cool! The news!" Gill exclaimed, rushing out of the room.

The Slammer rolled his eyes. "I gotta go. Maybe I can get out befowe they'we weady."

Matt walked out the door with him to sneak a peek. The moment the Slammer hit the elevator lobby, a reporter and her cameraman ran up to him. "Slammer! Slammer! Rumors are that you single-handedly saved a boy's life last Saturday night. Can you confirm or deny those claims?"

"No comment."

Gill jumped in front of the reporter. "Maybe I can answer your questions. I'm Gill Gillespie, talent extraordinaire!"

The reporter glanced at him and then turned back to the Slammer.

"Slammer, we know you are visiting a boy who was registered here in Enisburg Central Hospital for surgery. Was this the boy you saved last Saturday night?"

The Slammer and his pilot entered the closest elevator. The elevator doors shut, cutting the reporter off. The reporter and her cameraman ran down the stairs, probably to try to follow Slammer's helicopter with their news truck.

"One day I'll be rich and famous!" Gill called to them. "And then you'll be begging me for an interview!"

Matt chuckled and made his way back into the room. He walked over beside Lamar, who was standing at Nate's side. Lamar said he'd see Nate soon and then grabbed Alfonzo. They walked out to the elevators to calm Gill down.

Matt winked at Nate. "So you're doing all right."

"Yes. My hands and feet are warm now all the time, see?" He took hold of Matt's hand. His hand was warm and soft. "I'm going to become a basketball player like Slammer now that God gave me a strong heart."

He let go and pulled his shirt collar down. He looked under his shirt. Matt could see the very top of the stitch marks that ran down his chest.

"I bet you are," he said to Nate. Then, "Hey, you mind if I stop by over the next couple months until you get to go home? Would you like that? I'll even bring Alfonzo. He can give you some basketball tips."

"Yeah," Nate said. "He's *really* good."

"C'mon, Calhan," Hulk said, rising from his chair. "Nate needs his rest."

"All right," Matt said. As Hulk marched him toward the door, Matt turned and mouthed, "Bo-bo head" to Nate.

The boy giggled.

At the door, Matt stopped and turned to face Hulk. "Well, uh, I'll see you at school, huh?"

Hulk shook his head. "Ya just don't get it, do ya, Calhan?" His face turned hard as usual. "Nothin' changes between us just 'cuz ya tutor me or bring a star to save my brother."

Matt felt the heat rise in his cheeks. After all he'd done— after all they'd been through together—Hulk was still playing the bully. Sure, he had no idea just how much Matt really had done, but couldn't he give him a break? Matt had to know. "Why not?" he demanded. "Why can't anything change? Can you at least give me a reason?"

Hulk pointed a meaty finger in Matt's face. "Because we live in different worlds, Calhan. Take a look in the mirror. Listen to the tone of yer voice when ya speak to me. Until ya can get over whatever throne ya think ya live on because of yer smarts—cuz ya think yer better than me—nothin's gonna change."

Matt was speechless. What? *His* tone of voice? The look on *his* face? Matt felt his mouth dry up. Was he judging Hulk in the same way he thought Hulk was judging him ... seeing him as nothing? Matt managed to get out, "Hulk, I'm not on a throne, I—"

"It's another euphemism, Calhan," Hulk tossed back. "Man, yer just too far off to get it."

Matt slowly turned around like a wounded puppy, his tail between his legs. He couldn't find the words to respond. He had no idea he had been the one so far off ... the one who needed to run home. He wished he could pop open his laptop and fix everything in his heart against Hulk ... but, then again, he knew his laptop didn't hold the answer this time.

Matt closed his eyes as he exited. *God, I'm sorry,* he prayed. *Forgive me. Father, I need your compassion. Help me to be smarter in the way I treat others. Help me be smarter in the way I treat Hulk.*

Another three steps and Hulk's deep voice stopped Matt in his tracks. "Hey, Calhan."

Matt turned around and looked at Hulk, standing in the door frame.

"But, uh ... still ... I know what ya did. So ... thanks."

"You ... know what I did?"

"Yeah. I mean, if ya hadn't got Slammer and he hadn't got the heart ..."

"Oh, right. Well, I'm glad I could help."

"And, uh, I wanted ya to know . . . I got a seventy on my test 'cuz I followed yer advice on dat essay. Ya said I should write what I know, so I did."

"What'd you write?"

"Dat sometimes guys like me have lives full of problems. But if we could just catch a break once in a while—get a miracle—then it's like we don't got any problems at all."

Matt said a quiet thanks as he nodded. "How about that."

The moment passed as Gill's voice carried through the hospital halls. "I'm going to be famous!" he shouted. "Then the world will be like, 'Gill! Gill! Tell us all about you!'" Cracking a smile, Matt turned to see Gill at the end of the hall by the elevators.

"Man, don't you get a big head on us," Lamar said.

"Already has," noted Alfonzo.

When Matt turned back around, the door to Nate's room was shut. He took a deep breath and slowly made his way down the hall. "C'mon guys, let's go." The four friends entered an elevator and rode it down.

As the QoolQuad left the hospital, Matt tossed his backpack over his shoulder. When they stepped outside, a wave of heat hit them. Matt smiled and looked up at the twenty-story building. For a moment, he was sure he saw a small blond head pop up in one of the windows, bright blue eyes shining. But, then again, it might have been his writer's imagination, looking for that perfect storybook ending. No, Matt knew he hadn't solved all of Hulk's problems like he'd hoped he could. And he'd found a few challenges of his own to work through. Still, he had, at least, made things a little better. And that was what having an amazing laptop was all about.

Epilogue

"Are you *sure?*" Stan Calahan asked his son.

"Yeah, I'm sure. I want to go. It'll be fun."

"What changed your mind?"

"I don't know. Something."

Matt's mom squeezed his dad's arm. "Oh, you two will have so much fun! I just know it!"

"Are Lamar and Gill going?" Matt's dad asked.

Matt shook his head. "No, but Alfonzo and his dad are."

"Oh, good. I've wanted to get to know them better."

"Well, I'm going to bed," Matt volunteered. "I'm tired."

Matt's mom kissed him on the forehead and his dad gave him a hug. "Good night."

No sooner had Matt entered his room and changed into a pair of old shorts when his window burst open and Lamar, Gill, and Alfonzo fell into the room.

"What are you guys doing here?"

"You remember how we looked up Wordtronix. com," Lamar began, "to try and get more information about them?"

"Yeah. Everything listed was bogus, I remember. Dead end. So what?"

"So we looked up the other address."

"Other address?"

"The *other* address," Gill emphasized.

Matt's mouth went dry. "Oh. The *other* address." He remembered it well. He'd been there many times. When he had entered a search on the Internet for "Wordtronix," two addresses had come up: one for the Wordtronix company—which was totally bogus—and the other for a mysterious Web page. It contained just a cryptic note:

> If you've come here, then I must be dead and you must have the Wordtronix. I hope they don't find you. I've evaded them for several years now, but I know each day their search intensifies. They want their laptop back, whatever the cost.
> Don't be fooled. Their promises mean nothing.
> Trust me, I know. You have power in your hands.
> Wield it well ... as long as you can.

Matt had practically memorized it.

"So you looked up that Web address to see if there was any information listed about the owner?"

The three boys nodded.

"And?"

Lamar handed Matt a sheet of paper. A printout. It read:

```
www.civd.org
Registrant: Sam Dunaway (CIVD.ORG)
RR1, Box 87
Landes, AZ 87342
Domain Name: CIVD.ORG
Administrative Contact, Billing Contact:
Sam Dunaway sdunaway@CIVD.ORG
RR1, Box 87
Landes, AZ 87342
Technical Contact:
Administrator, DNS
administrator@CIVD.ORG
Record created on 19-Apr-1999.
```

Matt thought for a moment, then said, "Wait— Landes, Arizona. Where do I know that from?"

"The father/son retreat," Lamar announced. "It's *in* Landes, Arizona."

Matt's room was suddenly spinning. Everything was out of control again.

"So we're going with you."

"You couldn't keep us away," Gill said.

Matt swallowed hard. "Well, it looks like we finally might get some answers."

Introducing a fun, new CD holder for young boys that has a rubber 2:52 Soul Gear™ logo patch stitched onto cool nylon material. This cover will look great with the newly released 2:52 Soul Gear™ products. The interior has 12 sleeves to hold 24 favorite CDs.

$9.99 ($15.50 Cdn)
ISBN: 0-310-99033-5
UPC: 025986990336

Introducing a fun, new book and Bible Cover for young boys that will look great with the newly released 2:52 Soul Gear™ products. It features a rubber 2:52 logo patch stitched down onto nylon material. The zipper pull is black with 2:52 embroidered in gray. The interior has pen/pencil holders.

$14.99 ($22.50 Cdn) each

| Large | ISBN: 0-310-98824-1 | Med | ISBN: 0-310-98823-3 |
| | UPC: 025986988241 | | UPC: 025986988234 |

inspirio
The gift group of Zondervan